Diamonds on the Water

By

Kathi M. Gibbs

Eloquent Books
New York, New York

Eloquent Books
An imprint of AEG Publishing Group
845 Third Avenue, 6th Floor - 6016
New York, NY 10022
www.eloquentbooks.com

ISBN: 978-1-60860-399-2

Printed in the United States of America

Book Design: Roger Hayes

Edited by:
Ann K. Hills, Ph.D
Associate Professor of Spanish
Chair, Department of Modern Languages
University of La Verne
La Verne, California

Dedication

To Momma, whose loving grace inspired this story of selfless devotion and infinite loyalty to family.

Kathryn E. Mullin
Born October 5, 1918
Fink, West Virginia

Acknowledgements

To my "Sissy," whose confidence in my writing abilities stimulated the conclusion of this book.

Prologue

Sometimes in life, God creates extraordinary human beings that He places on this earth for the sole purpose of serving as nurturers. These special people, blessed by the heavens, possess an innate talent for benevolent compassion. They have the unique ability to assess the needs of others, and then provide essential care unselfishly.

Generally, the recipients of their magnanimous generosity are their own family members. They are parents, guardians or protectors of siblings. These caregivers grant undying love and affection without any consideration for their own well-being.

Regardless of the physical, emotional, or financial consequences, the dedication of these remarkable people remains unwavering. Despite the exhausting challenges faced by these caregivers on a daily basis, they place the welfare of others before their own.

Eventually, however, the plights of a caregiver traumatize their very soul. The challenge of providing constant care for others and ignoring their own wants and needs begins to take its toll on the deepest reserves of their existence.

These special people that inhabit this earth, *caregivers*, should be regarded as precious gems from heaven.

A Special Thank You To My Younger Sisters,—Debb and Kelly:

This prologue is dedicated to the two of you, for you are genuine caregivers in the truest sense of the word.

Chapter 1

I love the motion of the water as it gently rocks me back and forth with each wave. I love the smell of the crisp, clean sea air. I love the sound of the seagulls singing above me. Ever since I was little, it has always been my dream to be on the ocean, to have my own boat, and to sail the seven seas. I have read every book that I could that told of sailing or of the sea. My daydreams and this wonderful old swing take me on a journey across the oceans whenever possible.

"Annie, come on, supper's on the table. Stop yer day-dreamin' and git in here now! Momma, Annie's jes a layin' on that dang swing daydreamin' again." Irritated by my indifference to his beck and call, my brother Roy went back into the house.

"Annie, honey, come on in, yer supper's gettin' cold," Momma called.

Knowing that I had had enough daydreaming for one day, I gave into the hunger pangs in my stomach and replied, "Yes, Momma, I'm coming. What's for supper?"

"Ham hocks and greens with taters," Momma said with pride. "The dandelion greens are fresh and tender this year."

Momma and Papa sat down first at our huge, round, claw-foot oak table, which had once been my grandmother's most precious possession; the rest of my brothers and sisters (all seven of them) soon followed. I was the last to be seated, and since I was the eldest, I had the honor of sitting next to Papa.

It was Sarah's turn to say grace, so we all held hands. "Bess us old Lord for these shiny gifts, which can receive from you and yours Lord. Amen." Since we all take turns, the blessing takes on a new connotation with each of the children depending on their age.

"Looks like a fine supper, Mrs." Papa always called Momma *Mrs.*; "out of respect," he used to say. She smiled at him, quite pleased with the plentiful spread she had laid out for her big family.

"What's the celebration for?" Janey asked.

We were a poor family and our usual weeknight meal consisted only of root vegetables, beans from the pantry, tomatoes out of the garden and homemade bread. Very rarely were we served meat, unless it was Sunday or a birthday. With our large family—myself at age fifteen, Roy at thirteen, Janey, eleven, James, ten, Frank, eight, Elizabeth, six, Sarah, five, and baby Jacob, two,–there were many birthdays throughout the year. Nevertheless, we would always have chicken one Sunday a month and Momma would make a fruit pie. I loved those Sundays dearly.

"Well, your papa got a raise at the mill today, so I wanted to fix somethin' special."

Reluctantly, Papa said, "It's not much, only five cents a day, but it will help."

"Yay, Papa, good job," we all cheered.

"Not to change the subject, but what in the world do you daydream about, Annie?" Papa asked, obviously trying to do just that.

"Oh, she dreams about sailing!" James shouted out.

"Sailing? But Annie, you've lived in these hills of West Virginia yer whole life. What do you know about sailing?"

"I read a lot of books, Papa, and someday I *will* sail."

"Yes, when pigs fly, Annie," Roy said sarcastically.

"Roy, don't squash Annie's dreams. Dreams can come true if you want them badly enough," Momma answered.

"Don't encourage such nonsense, Mrs.; if she keeps her head in the sky instead of here on the ground where it belongs, she'll never learn any common sense, and that's what'll keep a roof over her head. She shouldn't be wastin' her time on such foolishness. In fact, she's fifteen and should be getting a job soon."

"But Papa, I want to finish school first," I pleaded.

"Why, so you can read more silly books about sailing?" he asked with disdain.

"We do need the extra money, Annie. Your papa and I have been talkin' about takin' you and Roy out of school this year so you can go to work at the mill," Momma said.

"That's great. I hate school anyway!" Roy was delighted but I suddenly lost my appetite. *How can they do this to me? I love school and definitely do not want to quit!*

"But Momma, you always said it was important to get an education. I can't quit now. I have the best grades in my class and only have two more years left before I graduate."

"I know, honey, but even with your papa's raise, we won't have enough money to even heat this old house during the cold winter months." Papa bowed his head in shame and I knew I could not say anymore.

"May I be excused, please?" I asked, as I got up from the table and went to my bedroom.

Supper was over, the table cleared, and Papa took off on our old mule Rex. Momma came into my bedroom crying.

"What's wrong, Momma?"

"Your papa was pretty upset; I think he went to Orville's for some moonshine."

"I'm sorry, Momma. I didn't mean to upset Papa, but it's just that I want to finish school more than anything. I will miss my teachers and my studies. I will miss being able to read all those wonderful books in the school library. I don't want to work at that dirty ole mill for the rest of my life. I have dreams and want to become someone special, someone important, someday."

"I know Annie; I want that for you too, but times are real bad right now, and since you're the oldest, you have to help support this big family of ours. Maybe you won't have to work there very long, just until things get better. Besides, you're a girl. They usually have girls sweep floors or other jobs that aren't so dangerous in the mill."

"OK, Momma," I said in resignation, "whatever you and Papa want me to do."

I cried myself to sleep that night, envisioning my days at the mill: coming home each night with black soot covering my face and saturating my clothes. I thought of all the fun I would miss at school and the encouraging words from my teachers. They used to say I had great promise and that with my scholastic achievements I could go as far as I wanted. I could become anything and go anywhere my heart desired. In the wee hours of the morning, I heard Papa bellowing outside my window. I opened my curtain and, sure enough, Papa had gotten into the moonshine at Orville's. Just as Momma and Roy stepped off the front porch, Papa fell off our old mule Rex. I could hear Momma say, "You old fool, you're stinkin' drunk! Come on, Roy; help me get your papa into the house."

As they tried to carry him in, I heard him crying. "Mrs., I don't want my children to have to quit school. I'm a failure as their father. I'm no damn good!"

"Hush now, old man. The children are sleeping and I'll have no more cursing, not in my house!"

"Yes, Mrs.," Papa responded in disgrace.

I went back to bed realizing that my quitting school hurt Papa even more than it hurt me. I had to do my part to hold this family together. After all, my family is the most important thing in the world to me.

Papa left for work before we all got up, and Momma was sitting at the kitchen table sobbing. "Momma, I've changed my mind. I want to help. I want to go to work at the mill. I can always finish school later when things get better."

"God bless you, Annie," Momma said, pulling me into her arms and hugging me so hard I could not breathe. The rest of the day was spent on chores. Roy and I milked the cow and cleaned out the mule's stable. Janey and James fed the chickens and gathered eggs. Elizabeth and Sarah pulled weeds from our vegetable garden, and Momma cooked and cleaned the house while Jacob was affixed to her side, hanging on dearly to her apron. After chores were done, all of us children were allowed to play awhile before Papa came home. Papa worked a long and hard day, but when he returned home he always had a smile and hug for all of us. Our family may not have had money but we did have lots of love.

While my brothers and sisters played catch in the back yard, I spent my free time lying on the swing. My daydreaming again took me on a voyage out to sea. I was at the helm of a magnificent ship, navigating my way through the English Channel, the Straight of Magellan, and around Cape Horn. Feeling the salty air spraying in my face and the wind blowing through my hair, I am taken away to a world that I know is out there–somewhere. In my daydreams, I never want for anything. Worries about money or anguish over the future are never a concern. All I sense is the freedom of the blue sky above and the ocean that surrounds me. Although my future was now gloomy, I still had my brilliant daydreams.

Off in the distance, I heard the mailman riding up our driveway. Janey and Roy raced to greet him. "What do you have for us today?" Janey inquired.

"Looks like a fancy letter from your Aunt Bess in Buffalo, New York."

"Momma, it's a letter from Aunt Bess," Roy shouted.

Momma came running from the house, obviously thrilled. She and Aunt Bess had been very close, growing up together in this very house. Ever since Bess had married a wealthy businessman and moved up North, Momma had missed her terribly. Once in a great while, Aunt Bess would write to Momma to see how we all were doing. She would write about her home in Buffalo and about the many travels her husband and she had ventured on. She and her husband never had children because of an accident Bess had suffered when she was very young. Since there was just Bess and Momma growing up, they had both longed for a large family. Momma always enjoyed getting a letter from her sister, although she felt a tinge of jealousy of the life Bess had away from these hills. It was ironic how they both were envious of each other: Momma, for the good life Bess had acquired, and Bess, for the large, loving family Momma had. I guess the old saying is true: "The grass always seems greener on the other side of the fence."

Momma sat right down on the grass where she was standing, ripped open the letter and began to read.

"What does it say, Momma?" asked Elizabeth. We all gathered around Momma, awaiting the news from Aunt Bess.

"She writes that the weather up North has been very rainy and cold."

"What else, Momma?"

"Hold on, children, let me read it through first! She says Charlie has taken ill with cancer and that she has had to go to work at his office to help take care of his business. Oh, listen to this, Annie. She wants you to come up and help her take care of him. They have a nurse that comes in, but she wants family to be around not only for him but also as moral support for her."

"I can't go to Buffalo, Momma; I have to work at the mill for more money," I replied.

"She says she will pay you twenty dollars a week!" Momma stated.

"Twenty dollars!" Roy exclaimed. "That's more money than Papa makes, isn't it, Momma?"

"Yes, indeed it is; in fact, I've never even seen that much money at one time," Momma answered.

"Wow, Aunt Bess must have a lot of money!" Roy added.

"Momma, I could send that money home to you and Papa," I declared. "That would help a lot, wouldn't it?" I asked.

"Yes, it would definitely help, but the thought of my baby moving that far away from home frightens me."

"Momma, I'm not a baby anymore. I'm fifteen."

"Annie, don't get all excited yet. We have to talk with your papa about this." Momma folded the letter up and neatly tucked it into her apron pocket. "Come on, children, back to work. We still have more chores to do before supper."

At dark, we heard Papa come through the front door. As usual, he gave Momma a kiss on the cheek and all of his children a big hug. He seemed in much better spirits today than he did last night. "What's fer supper, Mrs.? I'm as hungry as a bear."

"Black beans and rice, and I've made a blueberry pie for dessert."

All the children squealed with delight. "Blueberry pie, how wonderful!"

"We got a letter from Aunt Bess today, Papa. . ."

"Hush now, Frank," Momma interrupted, "let your papa get cleaned up and set down at the table before we tell him the news from Buffalo."

"I hope it's good news," Papa said. "I don't think I want any more bad news today. There's a rumor going around the mill that some workers are getting laid off."

Momma looked up from the stove in dismay. "We'll talk of that later. Besides, why would they give you a raise if they're layin' people off?" she asked. "Now go on and wash your face and change your clothes. Supper's nearly ready."

Once everyone was seated at the table, conversation began with the usual cordiality: How was your day? What did you do? Did you gather many eggs from the chickens? Then Papa asked about the letter from Aunt Bess.

Momma was a little hesitant, not knowing exactly how Papa would react, but just blurted it out. "She wants Annie to come to Buffalo to help with Uncle Charlie."

"She what?" Papa shouted. "What's wrong with Charlie?"

"He is sick with cancer and Bess spends most of her day running their business," Momma replied.

"I feel bad for Charlie, but that's impossible. Annie has to work at the mill come fall, and besides, Annie doesn't know how to take care of sick people," Papa responded.

"She has a nurse coming in each day to tend to Charlie's medical needs," Momma continued. "She just wants family to be around him and also to give her moral support."

"Well, that's just fine, moral support. We need her here for financial support," Papa snarled.

I spoke up finally. "Papa, Aunt Bess said she would pay me twenty dollars a week. I would send the money home for you and. . . "

Papa interrupted me. "I will not take her charity, twenty dollars a week, that's ridiculous!" –Papa then looked at Momma. "Did you ask your sister to help us? We are not a charity case yet; I can't believe you would go behind my back and ask her for money."

"I did no such thing, Mister!" When Momma called Papa "mister," we knew she was angry, so we all hushed. "My sister's poor husband is dying of cancer and all you can think of is your foolish pride. She's asking for our help, not the other way around. She needs Annie to help her get through this tough time she's been having. What on God's green earth is wrong with you?"

"But, the money. . . how can that much money not mean charity?" Papa said, trying to defend his position.

"That just shows me how much she needs Annie, and besides, she can afford it. We should let Annie go just out of the kindness of our hearts, but you must admit that twenty dollars a week would help us out a lot."

"Yes, it would," Papa submissively agreed. "Especially in light of that rumor I heard today."

"You said people will be getting laid off?" Momma asked.

"Well, I'm not sure if it's true, but I heard they're lettin' twenty people go 'cause profits are down."

"Any chance you may be one of those twenty people?" Momma asked with fear in her voice.

"I doubt it since I've been there over fifteen years, but you never know. Like you said, why would they give me a raise, just to lay me off? What about you, Annie? Do you want to go?" Papa asked.

"Yes, I do. It would be much nicer there helping Aunt Bess than it would be working here in the mill."

"You're right about that!" Papa agreed. He paused, and

then declared, "Well then, it's settled: you'll go to Buffalo to help your Aunt Bess. Agreed, Mrs.?"

"Agreed," Momma replied.

"Now let's eat this beautiful blueberry pie your momma made for us!"

I went to bed shortly after supper, but was not able to fall asleep. I laid there for what seemed like hours, contemplating my new adventure. I was assuredly excited about going to the big city and living in Aunt Bess's beautiful home. On the other hand, I was a bit apprehensive about going that far away from home and from my family. All my fifteen years of life had been spent in these hills of West Virginia, not venturing more than twenty miles from home. I was a country girl at heart. My grandiose dreams of adventure on the high seas were only that —dreams! Going from the country to a big city environment frightened me.

The comfort of home and its familiar surroundings had somewhat restricted my aspirations for the future. I had never thought of being anywhere but here in these back wood hills, living my life caring for a husband and our children, much as my mother had all these years. *Could I be successful doing anything else?* I wondered. After all, I could dream anything and everything as long as I was able to do so from this safe haven that was home, an asylum that protected me from disappointment, distress, and fear of failure. Without that security, would I be capable of accomplishing the goals and dreams I had imagined for myself? The answer to this question lay ahead of me. Regardless of the anxiety I was experiencing, I knew that my future was out there, waiting for me to seize it with an enthusiastic spirit.

Chapter 2

Momma wrote to Aunt Bess the following day. "I'm sure it will be about a week before she gets back to us. You'd better start packing a bag, Annie; Bess will probably send you a bus ticket for the trip as soon as possible."

"My first bus ride–I'm so excited! My first trip to a big city," I replied. After spending the entire night agonizing about the future, I had decided this trip would be beneficial not only to me, but also to my family. The money I would earn by helping Aunt Bess would definitely be put towards the family's needs here at home. How could I deny them?

"I want to go with you, Annie," Elizabeth said, starting to cry.

I picked her up in my arms and said, "I'll write to you all every day. I won't be that far away. Hush now or you'll get me crying too!"

"But I'll miss you, Annie," Elizabeth said, still crying a bucket of tears.

"I'll miss you too, Lizzy," I said while rocking her back and forth in my arms.

The next few days we waited on pins and needles for a letter to arrive from Aunt Bess. Finally her letter came. She was filled with joy that I was coming to Buffalo. I had always been Aunt Bess's favorite. She was with Momma the whole time she was giving birth to me, and she stayed with Momma and Papa an entire year before she met Uncle Charlie and moved away. She helped Momma take care of me. She bathed me, fed me, and rocked me to sleep each night. Momma used to say that we had bonded, and when it was time for Aunt Bess to move away, she was more upset about leaving me than anything else.

As Momma had predicted, Aunt Bess had sent a bus ticket for me. The cost of the ticket was five whole dollars and the date of departure was the following day. "Oh, my dear Lord," Momma said, "we have so much to do to get you ready." Momma spent the rest of that day scurrying about in a frenzy, making bread for me to take to Bess and homemade soup for Charlie. She believed that soup could "heal whatever ails you." She packed a bagged lunch for my bus trip and neatly stuffed it into my suitcase. When Papa came home from work, Momma told him I would be leaving for Buffalo tomorrow afternoon.

"I'll ask for time off from work. We'll all walk her to the bus stop together. Y'all meet me at the mill at noon and we'll go on from there," Papa said.

The bus stop was a good three miles from our house, a good long walk for all of us, especially the little ones. I remember sitting at the bus stop on my way back from school some days, just watching the people boarding and wondering what fabulous adventures they had planned. Now I would be the one off on an adventure of my own, to see what the rest of this world held for me.

Again, another sleepless night. *I wish I had a picture of my family to take along with me. I am afraid I will forget what they look like. Oh, nonsense Annie,* I thought to myself. *I am not going away forever!* I stayed up most of the night packing some of my most treasured possessions. I packed the heart-shaped stone James had found in the creek, the set of hair combs Gramma left me when she died, the windpipe Papa had whittled out of a pine branch, and the scarf Momma made for me last Christmas. *Oh my word, I will miss Christmas. How can I be away from my family on Christmas? It is our most cherished time of the year.*

Christmas at our house is celebrated throughout the whole week before and during the whole week after. Papa's journey into the woods—looking for and chopping down the perfect tree—begins the celebration. All of us children accompany Papa in search of our special Christmas tree and help drag it through the snow back to our house. Momma bakes fresh breads, rolls, and cakes for the Christmas Day dinner. All the finest canned fruits and vegetables she had put up the summer before are carried from the root cellar. The day before Christmas, Papa, Roy, and James go hunting for the biggest wild turkey they can find, while Momma and the rest of us make homemade decorations for the tree. Dried fruits and berries are strung together as a garland and the little ones cut out pictures from the magazines Papa brings home from work to hang on the tree limbs. Every year our tree is different and every year we think it is the most beautiful one ever.

On Christmas day, we awake to find gifts made from Momma and Papa's tender loving hands under our magnificent tree. On good years—financially, that is—the girls get new store-bought dolls and the boys get toy trucks or cars. On less fortunate years, Momma painstakingly sews homemade clothes for the little girls' dolls and Papa whittles wooden musical instruments for the boys. For Roy and me, we get restyled hand-me-downs from Momma and Papa. The rest of Christmas morning is spent at church two miles down the valley. After church, we head for home and start feasting on all the wonderful food Momma has prepared. Before bedtime, we sing carols and sit by our fire reminiscing about years past and dreaming of years to come.

The week after Christmas, we package up all our extra canned goods and deliver them to our neighbors, some near and some far. "The greatest gift of Christmas is the gift of giving," Papa would always say. I learned at a very young age that Christmas was not about material things, but the love we shared as a family. *How can I be away from home on Christmas? Maybe Aunt Bess will send me home for Christmas. I will ask her.* Finally resolved that all my ducks were in a row,

I drifted off to sleep.

Morning had come and I awoke bright-eyed and bushy-tailed, despite the fact that I only slept a few hours. Anticipation of my trip had me full of energy as I jumped out of bed and dressed in my special "go-to-church" dress I had laid out the night before. I pulled up my hair in a neat little bun on top of my head and went to the bathroom to wash my face and brush my teeth. Running downstairs, I tripped over one of Jacob's little toy trucks and stubbed my big toe. "What's the commotion?" Momma asked, dashing out of the kitchen.

"Oh, I just stubbed my toe," I replied. "I'm OK."

"Well, don't you look beautiful, Annie! But we can't send you to the city barefooted. Come in the kitchen, I have a surprise for you," Momma said with excitement in her voice.

I had not given thought to shoes, since all of us children go barefooted in the summertime. Just before school each year, Momma took us to the church in town to get our single pair of shoes for the school year. That was only if she couldn't repair the hand-me-downs. One time I had worn a hole on the soul of my right shoe and Momma patched it with several layers of old newspaper that Papa got second hand from the mill. At least once a week, Papa would bring home newspapers and magazines that had been thrown in the garbage can outside the mill's office. He always insisted on reading a newspaper every night. He said, "I don't want my children to grow up ignorant to the world around them." Unfortunately, however, most of the current events in those papers weren't so current; sometimes the news would be from weeks or months after the fact.

Even before the depression, our church would gather used clothing and shoes from the more affluent families in the area (of which there were few) and would sell them—for a "donation," as the church called it—to our communities' poor (of which there were many). We would spend hours trying on clothes and shoes. Sometimes, if we had extra money, we could even buy a coat for the winter. Mostly, though, the younger children got hand-me-downs, and Roy and I got Momma's and Papa's clothes they had outgrown from their younger days. We appreciated getting their hand-me-downs, even though they were a bit outdated. Although Momma wasn't much of a seamstress, she could sew simple apron-dresses for us girls. The boys' pants were reused repeatedly by applying patches made out of any material that was available. I remember once Momma had to patch a huge hole that James had torn in his britches right in the backend. The only thing she could find at the time was an old bath towel, which just happened to be flowery and pink. It took all she had to convince James that he had to go to school (with that flowery patch on his butt). Once there, at school, James was unmercifully teased. For the most part, however, only the girls were concerned with being in fashion, but Papa always maintained that being warm and covered surpassed being fashionable. "Fashion," he once said, "was only for the rich."

"When your Aunt Bess lived with us, she left a pair of her shoes behind. I have been saving them for you," Momma said. "Here, try them on!"

"They're beautiful. Thank you," I said graciously. Aunt Bess's shoes were blue satin healed pumps that matched the tiny blue flowers on my white cotton dress. Unfortunately, since my toe had started to swell, putting on the pumps was a might difficult, to say the least. Not wanting to hurt Momma's feelings, I stuffed my foot, sore toe and all, into my new pumps. "They fit perfectly," I said, grimacing.

"Oh my word, you look so grown up, I may cry. Come to the table and get some breakfast. You'll need nourishment to get you through the long day you have ahead of you."

I was hobbling to the table, still trying to sustain a smile, when Roy asked, "Why are you wobblin' around so? Haven't you ever worn heals before?"

"Sit down," Momma said, "Let me see." Jamming my sore toe into the shoe had made my whole foot swell and it now resembled a football. "That won't do, Annie, take them off right now."

"But I'm sure it will be fine, Momma," I pleaded.

"Take them off, Annie," Momma directed. "Roy, shave off a piece of ice from that block in the ice box and bring it here." Momma went to the sink and wet a cloth, then put the piece of ice inside of it. "Here, put your foot up on this chair." She then wrapped my whole foot in the cold compress she had made.

"That feels so cold, Momma!" I said, as the sting of the ice sent a chill up my spine.

"Just sit there; the swelling should go down in a bit," she insisted.

"But how can I get my things ready?" I asked.

"Just be still, we'll get all your stuff together," Momma said. "Children, after you finish your breakfast, go get washed up and dressed. We only have a couple of hours till we meet your papa at the mill."

Once breakfast was over, everyone started scurrying around and I, well, I just sat there like a lump. After an hour or so, the swelling had gone down and the throbbing had subsided.

"How's your toe now?" Momma asked.

"It's much better. See?" I lifted my foot, sore toe and all, showing Momma that the swelling had, indeed, diminished in size.

"OK, Annie, I'll have Roy carry your bag, but I think you should go without your shoes until you get to the bus stop," Momma said.

With Roy carrying my bag, Frank and James pulling Elizabeth and Sarah in a little wagon, Janey pushing Jacob in his carriage, and Momma and me in tow, we started walking down the hill towards the mill. I looked ahead of me and my eyes started to tear up; after all, this, I thought to myself, will be the last time all eight of us will be taking a walk together for a long while. I cherished our walks together through hill and dale, admiring God's handy work. This particular day I saw bright green grass carpeting the rolling hills dotted with patches of yellow buttercups. The sweet smell of honeysuckle that grows wild along our path permeated the air. I spotted a doe cantering across the field with her two fawns trotting behind her. I heard the sound of a flock of geese flying in formation above me.

"What's wrong, Annie?" Momma asked.

"I'm going to miss these hills in all their glory. Especially days like today when the sun is shining so brightly. Most of all, Momma, I am going to miss taking walks with this wonderful family of mine."

"I know you will, sweetie, and we will miss that too; but remember, this is a once in a lifetime opportunity for you, Annie. You are getting the chance to better your life," Momma replied with a tear in her eye.

"I know it is, Momma, but I'll worry about you, Papa and the kids," I said as I turned and embraced her, sobbing.

"Don't forget about the money you'll be able to send home and how much that will mean to us. Wipe your eyes now, we're almost at the mill. You don't want everyone to see you crying, do you?" she asked.

As I wiped my eyes, I could see Papa waiting at the front gate for us. "Y'all got here sooner than I thought you would." Papa smiled as he greeted us.

"You know how Momma hates being late for anything, Papa," Janey said.

"I was expectin' to have time to wash up a little in the men's room before we go," Papa said. "I'm as dirty as an old sow."

"Go ahead get that ole black soot off your hands and face, at least. We do have some time before we have to be at the bus stop," Momma said.

When Papa headed for the little washroom inside the mill, I reflected on how awful it would be to work at this dirty, disgusting place. Thick black soot bellowed from the smokestack, obscuring the sky for miles around. The plant itself looked so cold and foreboding. The sparse windows were smudged with soot and had cold steel bars imprisoning them. I had been here before at quitting time, and had watched the unfortunate souls who work here come piling out of the front doors as soon as the bell rang. Covered in soot from head to toe, with heads bent towards the ground, they walked downtrodden and exhausted towards their homes. Most of them had worked here their whole lives, and unfortunately, most of them will eventually become ill with black lung. My poor papa had worked here even before I was born, but luckily, so far this horrific disease had not afflicted him. As Papa again passed through the front gate, I realized how lucky I was to be escaping this place and a future doomed.

"OK, I'm ready; let's head off to the bus stop," Papa said as he took hold of Momma's hand.

It took another good hour to reach our destination. We walked together, hand in hand, through the grassy path alongside the dirt road. We climbed up and down other small knolls, stopping from time to time to pick wild flowers that were growing sporadically throughout the hillside. Papa suddenly came to a halt, bent over, picked up a tiny yellow buttercup, and said, "Come here, Annie. I want to see if you still like butter."

"What are you doing, Papa?" I asked.

He held the buttercup under my chin. "I did this a long time ago, when you were just a wee little baby. If your chin turns yellow, it means you like butter! See, I knew it! You must like butter very much; yer whole chin has turned a bright yellow." He laughed and so did I.

Finally, the bus stop was in sight, where my exciting future awaited me. My feelings of anxiety and fear had returned. What did I fear? Was I afraid to be on my own? I knew that I would be with family—Aunt Bess and Uncle Charlie—so that wasn't it. Did I fear the vastness and the indifference a big city presented? Was I afraid I wouldn't relate to the inhabitants of a big city? Did I fear my own naïveté? Did I fear. . . fear itself?

"Looks like we're a bit early. Let's just sit on these benches until the bus comes." Papa and Momma sat their weary bones on the roadside benches, while the younger children played around the little park area.

"Where do they find the energy, Mrs.?"

"We used to have that kind of energy when we were their age, but it's all gone now that we are old and decrepit," Momma replied.

"Speak for yerself, woman. I've still got a lot of spunk in this old body of mine," Papa said as he grinned at Momma.

"How's your toe, Annie?" Momma asked.

"All this walkin' has taken its toll. It's all swollen again," I said.

Papa bent over to look at my toe and said, "What in the world did you do, girl?"

"I tripped over one of Jacob's toys on the staircase and stubbed it. I couldn't even put on the new shoes Momma gave me," I said, rubbing my toe.

"Good gracious, how are ya gonna ride the bus? They won't let anyone on that's barefooted, you know," Papa said, concerned.

Just then, the bus to Buffalo pulled into the bus stop. I promptly slipped on my shoes, and instantly felt the pain in my sore toe start to throb. "It'll be all right. Once I get on the bus, I'll slip it off a little till I get to Aunt Bess's," I said in pain.

Papa and Roy helped me onto the bus, handed me my suitcase and gave me a hug and a kiss. Momma and all the children gave me a kiss and started to weep. "I'll be fine, don't worry. I will write to you everyday if I can. I love you all." I moved to the back of the bus where I could stretch out and was able to see my family as the bus pulled away from the bus stop. There they all stood, in line, waving and wiping their tears. I waved to them until my arm ached. Then they were out of sight. I loved my family so much; I could not believe I was leaving them. I started to cry.

Chapter 3

My sadness soon transformed itself into exhilaration, as I started to enjoy the picturesque scenery from my bus window. As familiar as I was with the hills of West Virginia, I scarcely perceived a change when we advanced through the abundant hills of Pennsylvania. The similarity was remarkable, with lush, green, rolling mountains and steep, curving roadways. Farmlands were scattered among the landscape with wide-open pastures that stretched out for miles. Oak, cherry, and maple trees, integrated with clusters of pines, dotted the hillsides. The farther North we traveled from the border of Pennsylvania entering New York State, the more the land seemed to flatten and the hills became diminutive in comparison. By the time we reached the outskirts of Buffalo, the skies had darkened. It was evening, but the lights of the city nearly replicated daylight. I had never seen so many lights nor so many buildings. I was overwhelmed! Lake Erie paralleled the city and the lake was filled with a great number of boats of all sizes. Fishing boats, sailboats, and tugboats were all heading in towards their respective docks at port for the night. It was positively breathtaking.

As the bus pulled into the station, I could see Aunt Bess waiting behind the turnstile at the front gate. Once the bus came to a complete halt, the welcoming relatives rushed to the opening doors of the bus.

"Annie, Annie I'm over here," Aunt Bess shouted as she

waved me towards her. She reached out her arms and gave me a hug. "I'm so glad you're here, Annie. How was your trip?"

"It was very long but I enjoyed it. Can I take my shoes off now?" I asked, feeling the pain in my toe starting to throb again.

She laughed. "Annie, as they say: 'You can take the girl out of the country, but you can't take the country out of the girl.' Can you wait until we are in the car?"

Blushing with embarrassment, I said, "OK." I grabbed my suitcase and started to hobble off to Aunt Bess's car.

"Oh, my poor dear, what happened to your foot?" Aunt Bess asked.

"I stubbed my toe at home this morning before I left," I replied.

"I'm sorry, I just thought. . ."

"I know what you thought, Aunt Bess, and it's OK. Let's just get to your car so I can take my shoe off. Oh, yes. . . Momma sent you two loaves of homemade bread and some soup for Uncle Charlie, here in this paper bag," I said as I handed her the large paper sack Momma had filled with goodies.

"How wonderful of your momma. I'm sure the soup will help your uncle feel better and I haven't eaten homemade bread since I lived in West Virginia," Aunt Bess said as she accepted her gift thankfully.

On the way to Aunt Bess's home, she asked her driver to slow down as she pointed out her husband's building and told me that I would visit there tomorrow.

"How is Uncle Charlie doing?" I asked.

"I'm afraid he's getting weaker day by day, but I know he'll be extremely happy to see you."

"I am delighted to be here. Thank you so much for asking me to come," I said excitedly.

"Thank you for coming. We both need your help." I saw Aunt Bess starting to tear up and there was desperation in her voice. I reached over and patted her hand gently and lovingly; just then, we entered the driveway that lead to an enormous home. "Well, here we are." Aunt Bess motioned to the driver.

"Russell, please carry Annie's bag into the house."

Russell had been in Aunt Bess's employ ever since she and Uncle Charlie had started doing well financially. He was a towering man, thin but muscular and rather quiet. The first week I heard him say no more than three or four words. I was somewhat stunned by his uncommunicative behavior, since I, on the other hand, came from rather boisterous kin-folk. I could tell, however, that he was completely loyal and dedicated to my aunt and uncle. I learned later that he was originally from Georgia and when the Great Depression hit, his family lost their farm, house and everything. He and his family moved to Buffalo and he found this job as Aunt Bess's driver and handy-man. Oh, yes, did I forget to mention he was a Negro, and as black as the day was long? Up to this point in my life, I had never met a Negro, but knew immediately that I would like him due to his kind and loving nature.

"Yes'm," Russell replied as he opened the colossal wooden front door.

"Thank you, Russell. Will you come in for something to eat? You must be very hungry by now," Aunt Bess asked. He nodded–graciously. I perceived she viewed Russell as one of the family.

The immense foyer had a marble floor and a magnificent chandelier hanging gracefully from the high ceiling at its center. Off to the right was a room Aunt Bess called the parlor that had tall, opulent windows that were draped in long, lacey curtains. The exquisite furnishings and elegant décor portrayed this home as one in which a lady of great refinement resided. On the opposing side of the foyer was Uncle Charlie's personal den. Each of the walls was covered with multiple shelves of books, more books than our school library held. I was ecstatic. An immense, round, oak table was surrounded by four oak chairs on one side of the room. On the other side of the room, there were two enormous leather chairs and a small table that held a tall reading light. I was in heaven.

"Aunt Bess, I think this is the room I love the most," I exclaimed.

"You must love to read. Come on, let me show you the upstairs and your bedroom," Aunt Bess said as she led me to a long, graceful staircase at the end of the foyer.

"This reminds me of the staircase at Tara in Gone with the Wind," I said.

"Oh, have you read that novel already?" she asked.

"Yes, and it has become one of my favorites," I replied.

As we ascended the commanding staircase, Uncle Charlie's day nurse greeted us. "Mrs. Brown, this is my niece, Annie, from West Virginia. She will be staying with us for a while," Aunt Bess said to the nurse.

"Hello, Annie. Good to meet you." Mrs. Brown was an imposing figure of a woman. She had short-cropped, silvery hair and striking steel-blue eyes. She was large in stature and looked impressively professional dressed completely in white from the cap on her head to her white stockings and shoes.

"How's Charlie this evening?" Aunt Bess asked.

"He seems in good spirits, Mrs. Goodman; I think he's excited about seeing his niece," Mrs. Brown replied.

"Well then, Annie, let's go see him." Aunt Bess directed me to the bedroom where Uncle Charlie was residing.

"Mrs. Goodman, I'll be downstairs preparing his medications for tomorrow; if you need me, just holler."

"Thank you, Mrs. Brown." Aunt Bess led me down the massive hallway and, just before we reached Uncle Charlie's bedroom door, she said, "Now I want you to prepare yourself. Uncle Charlie doesn't look the same as you remember him. He's been very sick these past few months and has lost a great deal of weight."

Uncle Charlie had always been, as I remembered, a very stout gentleman. His jovial personality had endeared him to all of us children. I remember when he was courting Aunt Bess; he always had pockets full of candy that he handed out to us. He would lift us up into the air and give us big bear hugs. His laugh was kindred to Saint Nicholas. His face was round and full, his cheeks were rosy, and his corpulent belly shook when he laughed.

"Hello, Uncle Charlie!" I swallowed hard. "How are you feeling?"

"Come here, my sweet little Annie, and give me a big hug," Charlie said in a weakened tone.

Feigning a smile, I walked over to his bedside. I was astonished to see the transformation that this horrid disease had made in Uncle Charlie's appearance. The once portly gentleman had now become nothing more than skin and bones. I leaned over and gently hugged my dear uncle. I could feel his skeleton protruding beneath his skin. I backed away in fear that I might hurt him.

"I'm just fine, Annie, and don't worry, I won't break," Uncle Charlie said as he sensed my apprehension. His once full cheeks had now sunken and the rosy hue had turned into a sallow, darkened tinge. "My goodness, Annie, you have turned into a young lady. How old are you now?"

"Fifteen, Uncle Charlie. How old are you?" Uncle Charlie started to laugh, but his laugh soon turned into a breathless coughing. Aunt Bess rushed to his side and called for Mrs. Brown. Mrs. Brown ran from downstairs and into the room, promptly lifting Uncle Charlie upright. She put a mask around his mouth and nose, and then turned on a monstrous machine that was situated next to his bed.

"I'm sorry, Aunt Bess; I didn't mean to make him sick. Is he all right?" I asked.

"Yes, he'll be fine; she's giving him oxygen to help him breathe easier." Once Uncle Charlie resumed normal breathing, Mrs. Brown administered his medication and he soon relaxed. "He needs to rest now," Aunt Bess said. "Let's go downstairs and get something to eat." Aunt Bess leaned down and kissed Uncle Charlie's forehead. "We'll be back later; you've had enough excitement for now."

I leaned over, kissed Uncle Charlie's cheek, and said, "I'm sorry, Uncle Charlie, I didn't mean to upset you."

"You didn't, Annie," Charlie said, still gasping for air. "I'm so glad you're here."

The moment we left Uncle Charlie's bedroom, I started to

weep. "It's OK, Annie," Aunt Bess said compassionately. "I know it's difficult for you to see him this way." We sat down on the steps of the staircase and Aunt Bess held me in her arms while I sobbed quietly. She lifted my chin and said, "You know something, Annie? That was the first time I've heard Charlie laugh in a very long time. You're going to be just the medicine he needs."

"But Aunt Bess, I made him start choking. I feel simply horrible," I explained.

"Listen, Annie, that was not your fault; he has coughing spells like that all the time. At least this time he was able to have a good laugh. Come on, now; let's get you something to eat. You must be starving!"

"I am a bit hungry," I replied as I followed her down the staircase and into the kitchen.

"This kitchen is huge," I gasped. "Momma would love to cook in this kitchen."

"I used to cook, but since going to work, I have little time to spend in here. We have a cook now and she prepared a little welcoming dinner for you. Please sit down." Aunt Bess motioned me towards the kitchenette in the breakfast nook. "We usually have dinner in the formal dining room, but it's past dinnertime now and the cook has gone home. I'll be serving you tonight."

"Serving me? At home Momma just throws everything on the table and we dig in and help ourselves."

"If I remember correctly, your momma is a very fine cook," Aunt Bess said as she set a plate of meatloaf, mashed potatoes, and peas in front of me.

"Meat? Is this a special occasion?" I asked innocently.

"Well, yes, this is a special occasion, Annie, but we generally have meat every night." Realizing the financial difficulty our family was having, she quickly added: "We have been blessed, Annie."

"Thank you, Aunt Bess. This is delicious," I said, digging in and eating as if I hadn't eaten for weeks.

Once dinner was over, Aunt Bess led me upstairs to my

bedroom. "You've had a long, exhausting day Annie. Do you want to take a bath first or go directly to bed?"

"I think I'm ready for bed, Aunt Bess. I am very tired." As we entered my bedroom, my mouth dropped wide open. "Oh my goodness, this is so beautiful and so big!" I gasped in delight.

The walls of the room had been painted a pale pink, the four-poster bed and the dresser were a cream color, and the bedding, canopy, and curtains were a deeper shade of pink.

"I hoped you would like it. We had it remodeled just for you," Bess said.

"It's absolutely gorgeous. I love it!" I replied in amazement. "You shouldn't have gone to all this trouble, Aunt Bess."

"Uncle Charlie insisted on the pink—he said he wanted it to be very feminine. We both want you to be comfortable."

"Comfortable? Good grief, I feel as if I have died and gone to heaven."

Recognizing that a sadness had overcome Aunt Bess and realizing what I had just said so callously, I tried to reprieve myself by saying, "I'm sorry, I shouldn't have said that, Aunt Bess. Its just that I've never seen anything this beautiful."

"It's OK, Annie, I knew what you meant. Come over here." Aunt Bess led me to a door on the far side of the room. As she opened the door she said, "This is your own private bathroom. What do you think?"

The bathroom was massive. It was painted the same pale pink as the bedroom and it boasted a white porcelain footed bathtub the size of Kentucky. The pedestal sink and dressing table were skirted in a fabric that was the same darker shade of pink as the bedding. "My own bathroom, I can't believe it. It's three times the size of our bathroom at home that is used by a family of ten. Oh, Aunt Bess, I may never want to leave here," I said, hugging her.

"You don't ever have to leave; we'd love to keep you here forever. Now get yourself off to bed. We have a big day ahead of us tomorrow. Russell brought your bag up here and put it on your dresser. Wash up and get ready for bed. I'll be up in a few minutes to tuck you in. You're not too old to tuck in, are you?" Bess asked.

"I'll never be too old for that, Aunt Bess, thank you," I answered.

Stunned by the beauty and lavishness of my surroundings, I sat on the edge of my bed, soaking in the advantages that having money affords people. I peered out one of the four windows in my room and admired the view of this entrancing city. The lights of the city had toned down and provided a soft, warm glow that stretched out towards the Lake. Suddenly I felt a twinge of guilt. How could I delight in this luxurious lifestyle, while my family was struggling so? I had only been here one day, and I missed them all desperately. I tried to dismiss my feelings of melancholy and proceeded to wash up in my beautifully decorated bathroom. *My own private bathroom, just for me! I still cannot believe it.* After washing up, I slipped into my worn, tattered, and slightly oversized nightgown that once had been my mother's. The warm familiarity of my nightgown made me long for home and family. I started to weep.

"What's wrong, Annie?" Aunt Bess asked as she came through my bedroom door. "Don't tell me you're homesick already."

"Just a little, I guess," I replied.

"Well, I brought you some warm milk to help you sleep. Now let's get you tucked in. I have a busy day planned for you tomorrow."

"Can we go to the lake, Aunt Bess?" I asked.

"Certainly, after we go to the office first. I have a surprise for you there."

"What surprise?" I asked.

"If I tell you, it won't be a surprise now, will it? I will tell you that it has something to do with a hobby your momma told me you have."

Reflecting on my long, exhausting trip and contemplating my days to come living in this lavish home, I pondered on the surprise Aunt Bess had for me. She mentioned a hobby that Momma had told her I had. What hobby do I have? The warm milk started to relax me and I soon drifted off to sleep.

Chapter 4

I abruptly awoke to the sound of the bustling city, sat up in my comfy bed, stretched my arms and yawned. I had slept semi-restfully. Remembering the dream I had during the night, however, sent a cold chill through my entire body. I had dreamed I was on a magnificent ship sailing the ocean, when, in the distance, I saw my family drifting on a wooden raft. The coursing waves of the ocean were throwing the raft backward and forward, and from side to side. My poor frightened family was holding on for dear life. I directed my ship towards them, but each time I came close to them, another wave would jettison their raft further out into the sea. Since they had no oars, Papa was desperately struggling to paddle through the treacherous waters with his arms, while the terrified children clung to Momma. I saw the fear showing on their little faces. I tried frantically to reach them, but could not. Then, just as another surging wave descended upon their tiny makeshift raft, I awoke. I lay there shivering for several moments before dismissing my dream as part of my being homesick and went back to sleep.

"How are you this fine morning, Annie?" Aunt Bess asked. "Did you sleep well?"

"Yes, I slept like a baby." Not wanting to recount my dream to my dear aunt, I devised a smile and asked, "When do I get to see my surprise?"

"You are a very impatient young lady, aren't you?" Bess asked.

"I'm sorry; I guess I am. Momma always said that patience was not one of my virtues," I replied.

"Well, then, the sooner you get up and get dressed, the sooner you will find out what your surprise is. Hurry, now. The cook has breakfast prepared and we don't want it to get cold. I'll meet you in the kitchen as soon as you're ready," Aunt Bess directed.

Shaking off the remnants of my dream, I proceeded to my bathroom, washed up, and dressed. Peering out of my bedroom window, I was immediately aware that this city was a completely different world to me. There were several people rushing by on the sidewalk below my window. Cars, busses and streetcars cluttering the roadway, all, I assume, were dashing to their drivers' place of work. At home in the country, the only morning sounds I heard were the birds singing and the wind rustling through the trees. Although I had always yearned for the excitement and the intensity a big city has to offer, hearing the noise that emanates from such a city made me long for that peace and quiet of my home in the hills.

"Good morning, Miss Annie," a cheerfully plump woman greeted me as I entered the kitchen. She pulled out a chair at the table, and said, "Please sit down, Miss Annie. My name is Maria. I'm the cook."

"Good morning, Maria. Thank you, it's very nice to meet you!" I courteously replied. *Momma would be proud of my good manners!* I thought to myself as I sat down gracefully.

"Would you care for some pancakes?" Maria asked as she placed a plate of food on the table in front of me.

"What did you call these?" I asked.

"Pancakes, Miss Annie. Don't you like them?" Maria asked.

"Oh, yes, I love them, but in West Virginia, we call them flapjacks."

Chuckling to herself, Maria positioned a dish of uniformly sliced butter, a pitcher of warm maple syrup and a plate of pork sausage patties on the table. "Flapjacks, you say. What a funny name for pancakes." I suddenly realized what a country bumpkin I was. I decided not to ask if she had any hominy and grits.

Aunt Bess soon entered the kitchen followed by Mrs. Brown. “Are you enjoying your flapjacks, Annie?” Maria and I both looked at Aunt Bess in astonishment. Aunt Bess laughed and said, “I haven’t forgotten where I’ve come from, you know.” She motioned for Mrs. Brown to have a seat. “Help yourself to the pancakes and sausage, Mrs. Brown; you’ll need all the strength you can muster today. Charlie had a bad night and is very irritable and cantankerous today.”

“Don’t worry, Mrs. Goodman, I can handle Mr. Goodman,” Mrs. Brown replied.

“Annie and I will be gone for most of the day; I want to give her a tour of the city and also need to go to the office for a while,” Bess said.

“Don’t worry about a thing!” Mrs. Brown assured her.

“I won’t. I know he will be in your capable hands,” Aunt Bess said confidently. Turning her attention to me, she said, “You must have been famished. You’ve eaten everything on your plate.”

I blushed, realizing I was sopping up every ounce of the maple syrup with the last morsel of flapjack on my plate. “Breakfast was wonderful. Thank you, Maria,” I said.

“Don’t you wish *we all* could still eat that way, Mrs. Brown?” Aunt Bess asked.

“Yes, indeed, but only the young can get away with that kind of appetite,” she replied.

In retribution, I said, “Papa always said that wasting food was like flushing money right down the john!”

Aunt Bess, Mrs. Brown, and Maria all started to laugh, and Maria said, “Your papa is a very wise man!”

“Come on, now, Annie. Russell has pulled the car around to the front and is waiting for us. Grab an umbrella here by the door; it looks as if it might rain again today.” As she turned to me, she asked, “Do you have a raincoat to wear?”

“No, Aunt Bess. All I have is a winter coat that Momma bought for me at St. Joseph’s Church back home,” I answered.

"Well, then, we might just have to go shopping today," Bess said.

"Shopping in a *real* store?" I asked excitedly.

Aunt Bess put her arm around my shoulder, smiled at me, and said, "Yes, my dear Annie, a real live store. By the way, how is your toe today? You seem to be walking a bit better."

"It's much better: the swelling went down and I can wear my shoes without it hurting too much," I replied. "Do you remember these shoes? Momma said you had left them behind at our house when you came up North with Uncle Charlie."

"Oh, my goodness, they do look familiar. However, they never were very comfortable— that's why I left them behind. Looks like we need to go to a shoe store as well," Bess responded.

"You mean to tell me they have a store that just sells shoes?" I asked.

Shaking her head and grinning at me, she said, "Come on, silly. I've got a lot to show you in this big city of ours."

Russell bobbed and weaved through the city traffic and finally came to Uncle Charlie's office building. "Here we are, Ma'am," Russell said as he opened the side door and helped Aunt Bess out of the car.

"Wow, look how tall this building is," I exclaimed with my mouth wide open. "If you laid it on its side it would be near as long as one of the ships I dream about," I exclaimed.

"Well, I never thought of it that way, but it is one of the tallest buildings in Buffalo," Bess replied.

"Does this whole building belong to Uncle Charlie and you?" I asked.

"Yes. In fact, Charlie's father had a small store here years ago and, since then, your Uncle Charlie has expanded the company and built on ten more floors. Our main office is on the twelfth floor," Aunt Bess replied.

"How do we get up there?" I innocently asked.

"Well, we could use the staircase, but I think I'd rather use the elevator." Aunt Bess led me to a set of double doors that had a half circle above them that numbered one through twelve. She pressed a button to the right of the doors and an arrow pointing to each floor came down to number one and the doors opened as if by magic.

"I've never been in one of these things before," I said apprehensively.

"It's OK, there's nothing to be afraid of. I go up and down this elevator twenty times a day," Aunt Bess reassured me. We stepped inside and Aunt Bess pushed the number twelve button, and the doors shut automatically. A sudden jerky motion made my heart fall into my stomach. In what seemed like a blink of an eye, the doors opened to the twelfth floor.

A little wobbly, I stepped out of the elevator. "That was sorta like sailing on a ship in my dreams, but instead of going side to side, we were going up and up," I said. "What an odd feeling!"

"You keep mentioning your dreams of sailing; I think we need to go to the drafting room first. I want to show you what we've been working on." Aunt Bess motioned for me to follow her.

"Is this my surprise?" I asked impatiently.

"Yes, my little Miss, this is your surprise." As she opened the door to a room filled with people working diligently at large tilted tables, she said, "Come over here, I want you to meet Joseph. Joseph, this is my niece Annie, from West Virginia. She has a passion to sail one day, and I want you to show her our latest project."

"Nice to meet you, Annie; as you can see this is only a preliminary sketch of your namesake." Joseph offered me a seat next to him and pulled out an enormous sheet of paper with a drawing of the most beautiful ship I had ever seen, in books or in my dreams. "As you can see the main mast will be over 50 feet tall and the overall length of this ship will be almost 150 feet. Although this rendition does not incorporate all the minute details, you can clearly see the name on the stern." Joseph pointed to the back end of the ship.

"Yes, it says Annie!" I said in astonishment.

"We named her after you at the inception of our plans.

How very coincidental that your momma told us much later how you daydreamed of sailing one day," Aunt Bess said, beaming with pride. "She's beautiful, just like you!"

"Oh, Aunt Bess, she *is* beautiful. I didn't realize you and Uncle Charlie built ships," I said with a sense of puzzlement.

"It's been a sideline of our construction business for only a few years. Your uncle has the same passion for sailing as you, so one day he decided to start building small sailboats and sold them to the locals for their recreational pleasure. They became very popular and soon, fishing merchants began asking Charlie to build fishing schooners. Before the Great Depression, we used to construct homes and buildings, but since then we converted our business into shipbuilding since the demand for housing had declined. With the onset of the war overseas, the demand for merchant ships and war ships has amplified."

"Aunt Bess, has Uncle Charlie ever built anything like the *Annie* before?" I asked inquisitively.

"No, the *Annie* was just a dream of his before he got sick. And although she's still in the planning stages, I hope to have her finished and on the water before Uncle Charlie passes." Sensing Aunt Bess's sadness, I quickly asked to see the more detailed drawings of the *Annie*.

"I have to run over to my office for a bit. Joseph can show you around here. I'll be back in a few minutes and we'll go shopping," Bess said as she excused herself.

I hugged my aunt, kissed her on the cheek, and whispered, "You will have a long time to finish her. I just know it." She held onto my hug for a long while, then turned and left the room.

Joseph took my hand, leading the way to the numerous drafting tables and said, "We all love your Uncle Charlie, Annie; he is the kindest man we have ever known."

I was amazed at all the workings and the detail it took to build a ship the caliber of the *Annie*. I was also quite taken with the fact that my Uncle Charlie and Aunt Bess declared this beloved ship to be named after me. It touched my heart deeply. I resolved that I would do everything in my power to help them with the bleak situation in which they found themselves due to Uncle Charlie's illness.

"Are you ready to go shopping, Annie?" Bess asked.

When I heard Aunt Bess call to me, I ran to her and hugged her. "I love you and Uncle Charlie so much. Thank you for naming this magnificent ship after me."

Again, she held onto my hug. "You are very welcome, my sweet Annie. I'm so glad you are here with us. Let's go shopping now." Aunt Bess said her good-byes to Joseph, as well as the draftsmen, and we headed for the elevator. On the way to the first floor, I bombarded Aunt Bess with a multitude of questions regarding the building of *Annie*. "How soon will she be built? Will you want to sell her? How many people will it take to sail her? Can I watch them build her? Can I sail on her as soon as she is in the water?". . . and on and on and on! I am sure Aunt Bess was delighted there were only twelve floors to descend.

"So many questions, Annie. Your momma was right about your passion for sailing. Whatever in the world created this passion in you?" I was amazed that Aunt Bess was actually intrigued by my interest in sailing—not at all like Papa, who viewed my daydreams as just a "waste of time," as he would say.

"I think it started when I read the book Moby Dick a few years ago. The power struggle between man, ship, and beast fascinated me. The problems of Captain Ahab and the ship he was sailing against nature itself filled my imagination to the point of actually sensing the emotional connection to the sea."

In amazement, Aunt Bess looked at me and said, "You know, Annie, I truly believe some people are put on this earth for a specific reason. I also believe that your propensity towards sailing—as it was with Charlie—will someday make your dreams a reality. You could very well become the next Christopher Columbus."

"Now you're teasing me, Aunt Bess," I bashfully replied.

"Not at all, Annie. You can become anything you want

and *do* anything you want if your passion is strong enough. But for now, let's return to land long enough to buy you some new shoes." We both laughed!

Chapter 5

Exhausted and wet after an afternoon of shopping in the rain, we returned home soaked to the bone but with packages from almost every store in Buffalo. "I'll have Russell take your new things up to your room and you and I can check on Uncle Charlie before we get something to eat. Are you hungry, Annie?" Aunt Bess asked, as she shook the residue of rain from her umbrella.

"I'm famished; I never realized how much shopping can work up an appetite." We walked up the stairs and into Uncle Charlie's room.

"Hello, ladies. I heard you went shopping and spent all my money today. Is that true?"

"Indeed it is. Annie needed new shoes and a few other things so we explored every store in the entire city for just the right wardrobe that would compliment your favorite niece," Aunt Bess confirmed.

"Well then, I must have a fashion show later. Deal?"

"Deal, Uncle Charlie. How are you feeling today?" I said in kind, as I leaned over his bed and gave him a kiss on the cheek.

"Much better now, since you're here, Annie!" Uncle Charlie replied.

"I also took her down to the office to see the surprise we had for her," Aunt Bess added.

"What do you think of your namesake, Annie?" Uncle Charlie asked.

"Oh, Uncle Charlie, she is going to be the most magnificent ship ever built."

"I think so too. I only hope I get to see her on the water before. . ." Uncle Charlie hesitated a moment, then said, "Before I get too old."

"You will, Uncle Charlie, I know you will!" Sensing Charlie's emotional reaction, Aunt Bess changed the subject and told him to rest a bit.

"We're going down to get something to eat, and then you're in for the grandest fashion show ever." She gave Uncle Charlie a kiss on the forehead and we promptly left his room.

"I only hope you're right, Annie; my dream is that he will not only be able to see his ship on the water but that he will also be able to sail her," Aunt Bess uttered with tears in her eyes.

"We need only to believe," I said reassuringly.

"Annie, you are truly a God-send to both of us. We will need to draw from your strength and positive attitude."

As we entered the dining room, Aunt Bess called out, "Maria, is dinner ready yet? Annie and I are starving!"

"Yes, Ma'am, I have scalloped potatoes and ham with a side of baby peas—one of your favorites," Maria answered. "Here is a hot cup of coffee for you, Mrs. Goodman. What would like to drink, Miss Annie?" Maria asked.

"Milk, please. Thank you, Maria. This meal looks wonderful," I replied.

As we sat down and started stuffing ourselves, Mrs. Brown joined us. "Did Charlie give you any trouble today?" Aunt Bess asked.

"He was a bit grumpy this morning, but when I told him you had taken Miss Annie to see her namesake, he perked up and smiled. He said Kate had told him that Annie had dreamed of sailing someday. He also told me the story of how you and he had met in West Virginia and how very much he adored Annie and the rest of her family."

"See, I told you that you're just the medicine your Uncle Charlie needs, Annie." Aunt Bess turned to me and hugged me.

"Now finish your dinner so we can show Uncle Charlie how pretty you look in all the new clothes we bought today."

As I dressed myself in the glorious apparel Aunt Bess had purchased for me, I stared at the full-length mirror in front of me. Back home I never had paid much attention to my appearance. If my face and hands were clean and my hair was well kept, I considered myself acceptable, although very plain, and that was good enough for me. Now, I stared at this young girl before me and gasped in disbelief. I am not sure if what they say is true— that the clothes make the woman, but I am amazed at the fact that I am no longer very plain. I saw that my tall, slim stature (which I usually described as being too skinny) fit quite well in these new accessories. Even though I had started to "develop" a few years ago, I had never really noticed the hourglass figure that I had somehow suddenly acquired. My long, dark, silky hair looked quite appealing when I wore it down over my shoulders. Back home I always kept my hair tied up, for it wasn't practical to do otherwise while doing my chores. My dark brown eyes seemed bigger and more optimistic here in this big city. I had to admit to myself, I was *not at all* just plain.

Aunt Bess propped Uncle Charlie up in his bed to get a better view of the parade of fashions. He smiled and nodded his approval to the collection of outfits I pompously displayed before him. At the end of the fashion show Uncle Charlie clapped his hands and proudly stated, "Annie, you are the prettiest young lady in all of New York State!"

I bowed in front of him and said, "Thank you, my dear uncle, for your kind comments and your money!"

Uncle Charlie laughed aloud, then said, "Don't forget, Annie, that true beauty comes from within and not from outside wrappings."

"I know, Uncle Charlie. Wearing these beautiful clothes makes me feel pretty, but I won't ever forget where I came from and that I am just a simple country girl deep inside. Thank you both so much for everything!" I said gratefully.

"You're very welcome, my dear Annie. Now off to bed

with you. You must be exhausted from your shopping excursion today," Aunt Bess said as she rearranged Uncle Charlie's pillows.

"I *am* very tired, but Uncle Charlie, would it be alright if I read to you from one of the books in your den tomorrow?" I asked.

"That would be delightful, Annie!" Charlie answered.

"Do you have a preference?" I asked.

"My favorite is Moby Dick. Have you read it before?" he replied.

I smiled at Aunt Bess and said, "Yes, it happens to be one of my favorites as well."

"Good, then, it's all settled. I'm looking forward to your reading to me. Goodnight, sweet niece of mine."

"Goodnight, Uncle Charlie and Aunt Bess. I love you both very much." I said.

Uncle Charlie looked up at Aunt Bess and smiled warmly. Aunt Bess hugged her beloved husband, saying, "I'll be right back, sweetheart. I want to tuck her in."

As Aunt Bess and I walked down the hall to my room, she said to me, "Annie, you have made your uncle very happy tonight and I know he is looking forward to you reading to him tomorrow. Thank you for such a good idea."

"Aunt Bess, would it be alright if I stayed up a little so I can write to my family?" I asked.

"Absolutely! If you get your letter finished, we can mail it tomorrow morning. Oh, by the way, I would like to give you a check for your first week's pay to put in the envelope," Bess said as she reached into her pocket and handed me an envelope.

"But Aunt Bess, I haven't even been here a week yet!" I protested.

"Let's call it an advance payment," she answered. "Besides, I've wanted to send money to help out your family for a long time, but you know how proud your papa is. Your being here is just the pretense I needed to give them help without hurting his pride."

"Thank you, Aunt Bess, that would be wonderful, but

you've spent so much on me already today!" I pleaded.

"What good is money if you can't make someone happy?" she replied. "I love your mother and the rest of your family dearly, and it truly breaks my heart to see them struggling so. It has been so dreadful for people during this horrible depression. Your Uncle and I have been so very blessed that our business has been virtually unaffected."

After Aunt Bess tucked me in and said goodnight, I reflected on my day and all the wonderful clothes she had purchased for me. What was it that Papa always said, "fashion is for the rich"? *Yes, Papa, you are right–fashion is for the rich–and how wonderful being rich can be!* I finished my letter and peered through one of my bedroom windows, glancing at Lake Erie. Night had again fallen and the city had darkened. The only light I saw was the moon shining across the water. Its reflection reminded me of thousands of glistening diamonds. If only I could send Momma these diamonds on the water, then she too could feel the richness life has to offer. Feeling homesick again for my family and a bit guilt-ridden for all the lavishness that had been cast upon me that day, I settled into my comfortable bed and cried myself to sleep

I arose with the sun shining through my bedroom window. The city was once again alive with the sounds of people bustling to and fro. Oh, how I missed my quiet, peaceful mornings in West Virginia.

"Good morning sunshine," Aunt Bess called as she jolted through my bedroom door. "I've been called to the office for a meeting. Maria has breakfast ready and Uncle Charlie is still sleeping. He had a very calm night and even slept through his medication time. Would you please check on him before going down to breakfast, Annie?"

"Of course, I'll be happy to," I replied, trying to wipe the sleep from my eyes. "Aunt Bess, I finished my letter to home. Can you please mail it for me?"

"Absolutely, I'll mail it on the way to the office. I'll see you later this afternoon."

I slept better, as well, last night! I dreamed of sailing the

Annie and having Uncle Charlie by my side at the helm. The two of us headed his magnificent ship out to sea with Aunt Bess waving from the shore. Just like Momma, Aunt Bess never really liked the water much, but had supported Uncle Charlie's dream because, as she said, "It makes him happy and when he's happy, I'm happy!" In my dream, I could feel the salty water spray against my face as the ocean waves rose up to greet the imposing sharp bow of our majestic vessel. To the starboard side of our ship, a family of dolphins was swiftly swimming in unison as if racing with the *Annie*. Watching them arch above the water's surface and then dive gracefully into the depth of the sea made me appreciate the intelligence and sociability of these wonderful creatures. So genuine and vivid were my dreams, that I was certain that some day they would become a reality.

Washed and dressed in one of my new outfits, I cheerfully trotted down the hallway to Uncle Charlie's room.

I knocked on his door and it was answered by Mrs. Brown. "Come on in, Annie. I'm just giving your uncle a lecture on eating."

"Don't you feel like eating today, Uncle Charlie?" I asked with concern.

"Oh, bother! Mrs. Brown insists I eat this breakfast before I take my medicine," Uncle Charlie said in a disgruntled tone. "Come over here, girl, I want to see you closer in your high fashioned outfit."

"I will, Uncle Charlie, but you mustn't give Mrs. Brown such a hard time. You know you have to eat something in order to keep up your strength," I said.

"Thank you, Miss Annie; I can't make this stubborn old man understand. Maybe you can get him to eat something," Mrs. Brown said in frustration while walking out of the room.

"She just wants to see me get as fat as I used to be, the old witch!" Charlie retorted.

"Uncle Charlie, be nice now. You know she only wants you to get stronger," I said sternly.

"I just don't have an appetite any more, Annie; it's

probably because of all these stupid pills I have to take," Charlie complained.

"I know, but would you please try to eat a little bit for me? Pretty please?" I pleaded. Finally conceding to my request, Uncle Charlie took a few small bites of his tomatoes on toast and drank a bit of milk. "There now, that wasn't that bad was it?" I asked teasingly.

"I swear you're as taunting as Mrs. Brown. Twirl around now, Annie, I want to see what a fashion plate you've become."

"Don't tease me, Uncle Charlie. You know I'm still just a little country girl at heart." I presented him with a smile that was a tad coquettish and he laughed.

"Boy, you're going to be a heartbreaker someday. I feel sorry for all the fellas that will cross your path, young lady. Annie, they simply won't have a chance in hell against your charms."

"Mr. Goodman, that'll be enough cursing out of you today," Mrs. Brown reprimanded upon returning to the room.

"The one last vice I have to indulge in and she won't let me get away with anything. OK – H.E. double hockey sticks–is that better?" Charlie said.

"Much better. Remember you must mind your language in front of a sensitive and impressionable young lady such as Miss Annie," Mrs. Brown answered.

"Don't worry, Mrs. Brown, I've heard a lot worse from my own father," I said. "Papa always said he wouldn't mince words: 'If your ears are too tender, then you shouldn't be a-listenin'."

Uncle Charlie laughed again. Trying to change the subject, Mrs. Brown asked if Charlie had eaten anything. "Yes, I ate some of this sawdust you served me," Charlie answered.

"Good then, now you can take your medicine," Mrs. Brown said as she handed Uncle Charlie at least six or seven pills for him to take.

"The only medicine I need is to have my sweet niece here," he said defiantly.

"U n c l e C h a r l i e," I scolded.

"Alright, give me those confounded pills," he said, and then turned to me. "You better get some breakfast yourself now, and don't forget, I'm looking forward to your reading to me today," Charlie said with a smile.

"How about right after lunch, Uncle Charlie?" I asked.

"That will be great! See ya later; I think I'll rest for a little while. Oh, Annie, I was going to ask you–do you have a boyfriend in West Virginia yet?"

"Goodness – no – Uncle Charlie, I don't have time for such foolishness," I replied.

Remembering that Momma was fifteen and already considered an old maid when she married Papa, I was sure that by 'country standards', and the fact that I had no inclinations toward boys whatsoever, I was most certain to die an old maid. However, there was a boy in my classroom named Billy whom I thought was somewhat good looking but much too immature for me. Besides, I had always been more interested in reading and my school studies than in flirting with any silly boy. Oh, how I would miss going to school. I would miss the camaraderie between my fellow students and the encouragement of my teachers. I had become what some might call a teacher's pet, since my grades were the highest in my class. I was diligent in my studies and conscientiously completed all work that was assigned. I never complained or grumbled about doing homework. I loved school. I loved my teachers. I was the *perfect* student.

I reached the bottom of the stairs as Maria was calling my name from the kitchen. "Miss Annie, come in for breakfast, your eggs are getting cold!"

"I'm coming, Maria!"

After finishing my breakfast, I went into Uncle Charlie's den to find the book I would be reading to him today. I was in heaven: all of Uncle Charlie's books were leather bound first editions. He had Shakespeare, Whitman, Mitchell, and a virtual plethora of famous authors. I looked through his wonderful editions of <u>Gone with the Wind</u> by Margaret Mitchell, <u>The Strange Case of Dr. Jekyll and Mr. Hyde</u> by Robert Louis

Stevenson, Othello by William Shakespeare and The Canterbury Tales by Geoffrey Chaucer—all beautifully bound in sumptuous, dark brown leather with their titles embossed in opulent gold print. Then I found it:–Moby Dick by Herman Melville! I sat at the big oak table and leafed through the pages of this wonderful novel. I wondered if Uncle Charlie's passion for sailing had been inspired by this magnificent novel, as had mine.

Knowing I had a few hours before reading to Uncle Charlie, I decided to take a walk outside and down the block. The hustle and bustle of this grand city was exhilarating, with automobiles speeding up and down the street and people rushing everywhere. The sidewalks were lined with trees whose colors were just now starting to change from lush greens to glorious reds and oranges. A sense of melancholy rushed through me as I reminisced about the beautiful hills of West Virginia and their magnificent autumn foliage. I would have been starting school about now. *I wonder if my schoolmates and teachers will miss me.*

Despite having my head in the sky, daydreamin', as Papa would say, I became astutely aware that my injured toe had once again begun to throb with pain. I bent over and took my shoe off to see if it had started to swell, when a bicycle came whizzing past me, knocking me to the ground.

"I'm so sorry, Miss. Let me help you."

Struggling to my feet, I replied, "Why don't you watch where you're going?"

I looked up to see this creature that nearly ran me over and found a boy about my age, with curly brown hair, emerald green eyes and rosy red cheeks. He was dressed in short pants (knickers, I think they call them), a white shirt with a brilliant blue knitted vest and a funny, floppy hat. He was staring at me with those beautiful green eyes and said, "I really am sorry, Miss. Are you OK? Did I hurt you?"

"No, I'm just fine. But you should be more careful," I scolded.

"You must have bent over just as I was passing you. I'm

sorry. Excuse my manners. My name is Michael O'Connor. Are you new here? I've never seen you walking here before. I ride to school everyday down this sidewalk and I was a bit late this morning. Which reminds me–I have to go! Again, I apologize." Off he went on his bicycle, then suddenly stopped again, and shouted back, "What's your name?"

"Annie," I answered.

"Just Annie?" he asked.

"For now, yes, just Annie will do fine," I retorted.

"OK, *just Annie*, nice to meet you. Maybe I'll see you here tomorrow morning."

"Maybe," I said coyly.

Realizing my toe was really beginning to ache, I turned around and headed back to Aunt Bess's house. At the driveway entrance, I saw Russell opening the car door for Aunt Bess and I waved.

"Where have you been, Annie?" Aunt Bess asked.

"Just for a short walk down the block. I met a boy. He ran me down with his bicycle," I said.

"My dear Annie, you have to be more careful in talking to strangers in this city," she said, obviously concerned for my welfare.

"But he was very polite and he did apologize. He was also very cute!" I said, blushing.

"What's this, you're here only a short time and you have a boyfriend already?" she asked.

"I didn't say he was my boyfriend, I just said he was cute. For goodness sake, Aunt Bess, you sound like Uncle Charlie now," I replied.

"Um!" Aunt Bess had a smirk on her face, then said, "Come on inside. I want to show you what I brought from the office."

She put her arm around my shoulder as we walked into the house. "I hope your Uncle Charlie is awake. I brought home some of the blueprints of *Annie* for him to approve. Joseph has suggested that we use colored sailcloth for the main mast."

"How beautiful that would be! What color are you thinking about?" I asked.

"I'm not sure. I was thinking of a brilliant red or a deep navy blue. I want to see what Charlie thinks about it, since traditionally white has always been used for sails."

Just as we reached the staircase, Mrs. Brown came running down. "Mrs. Goodman, hurry, Mr. Goodman is having a terrible spell." When we reached Uncle Charlie's bedroom, we could see that he was gasping for air and his face was turning a putrid shade of gray.

"Mrs. Brown, go call the doctor. We're taking him to the hospital. Annie, get Russell to bring the car around the front and then have him come up here to help us."

While Mrs. Brown and I raced down the staircase, almost tripping over each other in a panic, Aunt Bess went to Uncle Charlie's bedside and tried to calm him. I soon returned with Russell. Mrs. Brown swiftly unhooked Uncle Charlie's air machine as Russell picked him up in his arms and carried him gently to the car.

"Do you want to stay here with Maria, Annie?" Aunt Bess asked.

"Absolutely not, I'm going with you!" I answered.

Thank God, the hospital was only a few blocks away. As soon as we pulled into the emergency area, three men in white coats came running towards the car. They helped Russell put Uncle Charlie on a gurney and then sped him through the doors of the hospital. Aunt Bess, Mrs. Brown, and I followed close behind. Once in the emergency room, the doctors started hooking Uncle Charlie up to all kinds of machines. Monitors began beeping, lights started blinking, and doctors and nurses were scurrying about trying to stabilize Uncle Charlie's condition. One nurse came over and told us we had to stay outside in the waiting room. "I'll come to get you when we get Mr. Goodman settled," she said.

As we sat down in the waiting area, Aunt Bess took my hand. I could feel she was shaking. She said, "We've gone through this so many times. One of these times will be the last."

"Aunt Bess, please don't say that. He will be fine, I just

know it," I said reassuringly.

"Oh, Annie. I'm so glad you're here with me." She trembled as she started to cry.

I put my arms around her and hugged as hard as I could, but I did not know what to say to calm her trembling. "Mrs. Brown, can you get some coffee for Aunt Bess, please?"

"I'll be right back with some; do you want anything, Annie?" Mrs. Brown asked.

"No thank you, I'm fine," I replied.

At least an hour had passed before the nurse came out and announced, "You can see him now." I helped Aunt Bess to her feet and we went in to see Uncle Charlie. I was in shock when I saw that Uncle Charlie was connected to wires and tubes coming in and out of his body. They had put a breathing tube down his throat and an IV in both his arms. The color in his cheeks had returned somewhat but his eyes were closed.

"Is he sleeping?" I asked the doctor.

"Yes, we gave him a sedative so he can sleep. He had a severe spell but he is stable now. Unfortunately, I believe the cancer is becoming more aggressive now. Mrs. Goodman, I will need to keep him in the hospital a few days to do some testing," the doctor said.

"Of course, whatever you need to do," Aunt Bess replied.

We sat by Uncle Charlie's bedside well into the evening hours. Around 8:00 p.m., the doctor came into the room, checked Charlie's vitals, and said, "You should all go home now and get some rest. He will be sleeping through the night. I'll call you when he wakes in the morning."

"No, I want to stay with him," Aunt Bess said.

"You need your sleep too, Aunt Bess," I pleaded. "Please come home with us."

"I guess you're right, Annie." Aunt Bess then kneeled down beside Uncle Charlie's bed and recited a prayer. Mrs. Brown and I joined her. After our prayer, Aunt Bess leaned over and kissed Uncle Charlie gently on his forehead, and we left the hospital.

Chapter 6

Days turned into weeks and weeks turned into months; Uncle Charlie's cancer had progressed rapidly. The doctors had kept him in a constant testing and treating mode at the hospital. Exhaustion was starting to show on Aunt Bess. She and I spent almost every waking moment of the day by Uncle Charlie's bedside. One morning, at approximately 4:30, the hospital called and reported Uncle Charlie had taken a turn for the worse. Aunt Bess woke me and asked me to go to the hospital with her. As Russell drove us to the hospital, Aunt Bess was sobbing and quivering. I tried to console her, but I was not sure of what was happening at this point. The thought of losing Uncle Charlie scared me. I had never lost anyone close to me except for Gramma, who died when I was only four years old. Death has always terrified me. What happens when you die? Does your soul really go to heaven as Momma had always told me? Or, on the other hand, is death just simply. . . the end? I did not understand death at four years of age; at fifteen, I still did not!

Once at the hospital, Aunt Bess refused to get out of the car. "I'm afraid I am losing my husband, my dear Charlie. I don't want to go in there!"

"Aunt Bess, you're not alone. I'll be with you," I said in calming tone.

"Mrs. Goodman, please come this way." The doctor greeted Aunt Bess at the entrance. "Mr. Goodman has been asking to see you and his niece."

Aunt Bess held my arm tightly as we walked into Uncle Charlie's room. He looked horrid. The grayish color had returned to his face and his chest was heaving in an effort to breathe. Three nurses and the doctor were at his side adjusting all the contraptions to which he was connected.

"Charlie, I'm here." Aunt Bess ran to his side and kissed his forehead.

"Where's Annie?" Uncle Charlie gasped and tried to lean forward.

"She's here, but you mustn't try to talk, Charlie," his dear wife commanded. "Save your strength." Aunt Bess reached for his hand and felt it was cold and dry. She knew, however, that if her husband had something to say, nothing on this earth would stop him!

"Bessie, I want our wonderful niece to own and sail her namesake, the *Annie,*" he whispered. I looked up at Aunt Bess in surprise and she simply shook her head in agreement.

"But Uncle Charlie, you will sail her yourself when you get well again," I said with tears filling my eyes.

"No I won't, child. I cannot fight this anymore! I want you to promise me you will fulfill your dreams to sail the seven seas."

"Of course I will, but. . ." Aunt Bess took hold of my hand and pressed it against Uncle Charlie's cheek.

"Do as your uncle tells you, Annie," Aunt Bess said, with her eyes full of tears.

With tears now streaming down my face, I replied, "I will, Uncle Charlie, but in my heart you own the *Annie* and you will always be at the helm with me."

"One more thing; promise me you'll take good care of your Aunt Bess," Charlie said.

"I will, Uncle Charlie. I love you." I stepped back and Aunt Bess put her arms around her beloved husband.

"Charlie, thank you for being my husband. I love you."

The monitors stopped beeping and a flat line appeared on the screen. My dear, sweet Uncle Charlie was gone.

The days following the funeral were filled with overwhelming sadness. Aunt Bess cried relentlessly for days on end. During the funeral ceremony, she had put up a remarkable façade for all the attendants that came to pay their respects. At Charlie's wake, she seemed strong and in charge. Amazingly, she had held her composure until all the arrangements were complete and the last well-wisher had left the house. Once peace and quiet had returned to the home that she and Charlie had occupied for so many years, she began to fall apart. Despite my urging, Aunt Bess secluded herself in her bedroom, refusing to see anyone—not even me! She barricaded herself in the room where Uncle Charlie had laid ill for so many months and would not even come out to eat. On several occasions, I had called Mrs. Brown to the house to see if she could help, but Aunt Bess refused to see her. Each time I went into Aunt Bess's room to plead with her to come down to eat, she would just hold me close to her, rocking back and forth sobbing mournfully. I felt I had failed her in her time of need.

Not knowing what else to do, I wrote to my mother asking her to come to Buffalo. She, of course, agreed, but said it would take a few days for her to arrange having someone tend to the children while she was gone. As soon as I knew she was coming, I asked Joseph from the office to make the necessary travel arrangements for my mother. Concerned for Aunt Bess's welfare also, he immediately purchased a bus ticket and sent it through the mail by special delivery.

The following week my mother arrived at the Buffalo bus station. Not wanting to leave Aunt Bess alone, I had Russell pick up Momma.

"Momma, I'm so happy to see you. I missed you so much. How are Papa and the kids?"

"Everyone's fine, Annie. How are you?" she asked.

"I'm OK, but I'm so worried about Aunt Bess. She hasn't come out of her room and hasn't eaten in days," I replied.

"Take me to her," Momma commanded.

As I led Momma upstairs to where Aunt Bess had sequestered herself, I asked, "Momma, how are you doing money-wise? Have you been getting the twenty dollars I've sent to you?"

"Yes, and it has been a god-send since your father was laid off from the mill," she replied.

"What? When did that happen?" I asked.

"Just a few weeks ago, but we'll talk of that later, Annie. Right now I have to talk some sense into that sister of mine."

"Aunt Bess," I called as I knocked on her door. "I have a visitor here to see you."

"Go away! I don't want to see anyone!" she shouted.

Momma, in her take-charge manner, barged through the door and said, "You will see me and you will listen to everything I tell you! And that's that!"

"Kate!" Aunt Bess shrieked. "I never thought in a million years that I would see you out of West Virginia and here in Buffalo."

"This city is noisy, dirty, and has too many people buzzing around. Now I remember why I don't like big cities." Momma ran to her sister's bedside and hugged her dearly. "Now what in the world are you doing in bed at 2 o'clock in the afternoon? Have you become a lazy woman?"

"I can't seem to find the energy for day-to-day living since Charlie passed away," Bess replied.

"I'm so sorry about Charlie." Momma paused, blessed herself, and said, "God rest his kind soul. Nevertheless, Bess, your life must go on, and you have your business to run. All those people who work for you are counting on you and, most importantly, you have my wonderful daughter Annie who has been worried sick about you."

"I know I've been selfish. I'm sorry." Aunt Bess lowered her head in shame. "It's just that Charlie was my whole life, my only reason for living. Without him I have nothing."

I quickly spoke up: "That's just not true, Aunt Bess. You have Russell and Maria. You have Joseph and all the people at your company, and you have a ship to finish building. Remember that you promised Uncle Charlie. Besides, you have me, and if it's alright with Momma and Papa, I'd like to stay here with you as long as you'll have me."

"Annie's right, Bess, you have a lot to live for. I think it's a good idea for her to stay with you if you want," Momma said.

Aunt Bess sat upright on the edge of her bed, put her face in her hands, and started weeping uncontrollably. "I've been so horrible to everyone, especially to you, Annie. I am so sorry. Please forgive me."

Momma and I sat next to Aunt Bess on her bed and hugged each other. "Of course we forgive you, we love you. All of us love you!" I said.

"OK now, lazy bones, get up out of that bed and get dressed. You're going to show me this nasty ole city of yours," Momma demanded.

"You have always bossed me around, even when we were kids," Aunt Bess replied.

"That's because I'm older than you!" Momma said. "Now do as I say! We'll be waiting for you downstairs."

When Aunt Bess approached the top of the stairs, she was amazed to see an assembly of her dearest companions. Russell, Maria, Mrs. Brown, Momma, and I were at the bottom cheering her on. Mrs. Brown called out, "Good to see you up and around, Mrs. Goodman."

"Please call me Bess! I want all of you to call me Bess from now on, except for you, Annie; you can still call me *Aunt* Bess."

Momma and I took Aunt Bess by the arms and led her into the kitchen. "Look what Maria has made for you! It's your favorite: pork chops and applesauce."

Once Aunt Bess and I took Momma for a grand tour of Buffalo, we headed for Charlie's office building to show her the grand finale–the *Annie*! It took at least fifteen minutes to convince Momma to get in the elevator. I thought she was going to be sick when it started moving upward. Aunt Bess proudly introduced her sister to all the workers and then showed her the blueprints for the grand ship she was building. "This was Charlie's pride and joy. A life-long dream of his was to sail her around Lake Erie and beyond. He left his magnificent ship, once it is built, to Annie."

Momma looked at Bess and then at me. "Annie, this is your daydream!"

"Yes, Momma, isn't she a beauty?" I said.

Momma smiled and hugged me. It was likely that she had never seen me so happy and excited. She must have decided right then that she would not tell me of the misfortune that had befallen the family: she would not talk of Papa losing his job or of the cancerous mass the doctor had found in her breast. Her daughter's happiness was more important and she could not (or would not) ruin it.

A few days had passed and, unfortunately, it was time for Momma to return home.

"I have had Mrs. Johnson looking after Sarah and Jacob during the day when the rest of the children are in school. And of course, your papa is with them all at night. I must get back before they learn they can do without me."

"That will never happen, Kate. I'm sure they miss you terribly," Aunt Bess said.

"Momma, did you say that Papa was laid off from the mill?" I asked.

"Yes, but it's only temporary. I'm sure he'll be back to work soon. Don't worry," Momma replied.

When Russell drove us all to the bus station, I felt as if my heart was being torn into pieces. I wanted to return home with Momma and see my beloved family, but I also wanted to stay with Aunt Bess. Since Aunt Bess was alone now, I decided she needed me more. Besides, whatever money I would make here, I would continue to send home to my family. Before we reached the gate, Aunt Bess gave me a nudge and said, "I slipped some money in your momma's pocket. Don't tell her."

"Thank you, Aunt Bess. I know she will need it since Papa isn't working right now," I said appreciatively.

"Yes, that's what I figured," Bess said. Tears and waves of good-bye followed kisses and hugs as Momma's bus sped onto the highway.

Chapter 7

Kate leaned back against the seat on the bus and mentally recounted the visit with her daughter and her sister. She thought to herself, what a wonderful, caring daughter her Annie was. She was beaming with pride when she remembered how mature her daughter had appeared to be. She had grown into a beautiful, loving woman. She recognized that her dreams for Annie would someday, unquestionably, become reality.

As her bus pulled up to the bus stop near home, she reached into her pocket to retrieve a tissue and found a wad of money. Ones, tens, and even a twenty-dollar bill were all rolled up neatly and secured with a rubber band. She nearly passed out at the sight of so much money. *God bless you, Bess*, she said to herself, and quickly tucked the money into her purse. Her husband John and all the children were at the bus stop, eagerly awaiting her return.

"Momma, Momma" they all cried, running toward her in sheer excitement.

"Welcome home. We missed you," her husband said as he put his arms around her.

She was glad to be home, for she had missed them too. As she looked at her family, she realized that despite the trials and tribulations, her family was the only thing in the world she truly cherished. She also felt quite pleased that she had not revealed to her daughter Annie all the unfortunate circumstances that had overtaken this family. She felt in her heart that at least one of her offspring would be able to rise above the troubles and hardships of being poor.

She had not spoken of her visit to the doctor with anyone in her family. When she had gone into the town of Weston in the guise of grocery shopping on that chilly afternoon a month ago, she knew something was wrong. She had felt a lump beneath her right breast when she had been washing up one morning. At first, she thought nothing of it, until it started to grow larger. Knowing her husband was out of work and no longer had insurance coverage, she prayed the mass would go away on its own. However, it had not. The doctor had told Kate that she would need an operation to remove her right breast.

"John just got laid-off from work. We don't have any insurance to cover the costs of an operation," she had told Dr. Mead.

"Kate, if you don't have it removed it will continue to grow and spread." Dr. Mead never was one to mince his words. He had always been straightforward with Kate all through their doctor-patient relationship. "Please consider your options here. If you have your breast removed, your chances of survival are good. If you don't have it taken care of, your chances go down to zero."

"I'll have to talk it over with John. I'll get back to you."

"Don't wait too long, Kate. You have a big family that is counting on having you around for a long time."

"I know." Kate bowed her head as she left Dr. Mead's office. She knew all too well the consequences of cancer, for her mother had died from uterine cancer when she was only forty-eight. At that time, with no treatment available, her mother suffered a horribly painful death.

Kate was waiting for just the right time to talk with her husband about the cancer. Unfortunately, the right time never presented itself. Then when Annie had called her to Buffalo for Aunt Bess, Kate put aside her quandary to rush to her sister's side. Now that she was back at home, she would talk to John.

On the walk back to their modest little home, John told Kate that his chances of getting back to work were impossible since the company who owned the mill was going out of business completely. He told her he had been looking for work in Weston but times were so tough that no one was hiring.

Since Roy had already quit school to work in the mill, he had taken a part-time job at the grocery store in Weston bagging groceries. With the exception of the twenty dollars Annie was sending to them each week, Roy's meager pay of two dollars a day was the only income the family had. John looked dolefully at Kate and said, "I feel like I failed you and the kids."

"My dear husband, please don't be upset. Something will come up—I just know it will. I could take in laundry and we could sell some of Grammas' furniture. We'll get by, you'll see."

"Not a very nice homecoming for you, is it Kate?" her husband asked.

"I'm glad to be home with my sweet family," Kate said as she kissed him on the cheek.

Knowing the desperation her husband was experiencing, she had not the heart to burden him with her medical problems. *I will tell him when things get back to normal,* she thought to herself.

As the days and weeks went by, Aunt Bess became engulfed in the business that was now her own. She worked diligently hour after hour, day after day, continuing the business of erecting office buildings in downtown Buffalo. Her business also expanded to the suburban area where new homes were now in demand. She worked tirelessly around the clock without taking time out for herself (or me). I was beginning to feel that Aunt Bess did not need me anymore. In fact, I was not even sure she knew I was still around, until one day, over breakfast, when she asked, "Annie, what do you think about going back to school?"

"Oh, Aunt Bess, could I?" I asked.

"Buffalo has two or three very nice high schools; I think

it's time for you to finish your education. Your momma said you were doing very well and had good grades back home in school," Bess stated.

"I loved school and would love to go back. The only reason I quit school was to help my family. If I go back to school, I won't be able to send them any money."

"Why not? My company has been doing very well financially; in fact, I'm thinking of giving you a raise."

"A raise? I don't do anything now for the money you give me, Aunt Bess."

"You most certainly do. You help Maria around the house and you're good company for me," Aunt Bess said with a smile.

"Oh, Aunt Bess, you are the greatest aunt in the world. I love you so much!"

"Then it is settled," she said. "After breakfast, we will go to the high school downtown and sign you up for the second half of this year. Annie, I want to apologize to you for not showing you more attention lately. It's just that the success of Uncle Charlie's business is very important to me. Charlie's friend once said, 'Every great architect is—necessarily—a great poet. He must be a great original interpreter of his time, his day, his age.' That friend was Frank Lloyd Wright. As your dream has always been to sail, mine has been to become a great architect, and to design buildings like the D.D. Martin House and the Larkin Building here in Buffalo."

"I understand, Aunt Bess. You need not apologize to me. It was good for you to plunge yourself into your work, and I certainly understand dreams. That is why I appreciate you letting me go back to school. Dreams can only be fulfilled through knowledge," I replied.

I enrolled in one of the finest schools in Buffalo and, within the remaining school year, I had passed all the required testing with honors and was eligible for graduation the following spring. Throughout the rest of that year, I had developed a few lifelong friendships; one especially was the bond that formed between Michael and I. Yes, Michael

O'Connor, the boy who ran me over with his bicycle had become my dearest friend. We became inseparable, going to the movies, eating dinner at his house and mine, and studying together almost every night after school. Aunt Bess once said, "Be nice to Michael. He is a nice boy from a good family. Besides that, I think he has a crush on you." I, however, only saw Michael as a friend and nothing more.

It was graduation day, and the auditorium was filled to capacity. I was back stage nervously reading over the speech I was to make, as Valedictorian. "I don't see them, Michael," I said as I peeked through the curtain.

"It's early yet. Your family said they would be here, and I'm sure they will be," he replied.

"How do I look?" I asked. "I'm so nervous I'm getting sick to my stomach." Michael took hold of my shoulders. "You're beautiful. You are absolutely beautiful, Annie!" He then leaned towards me, kissed me square on the lips, and said, "I've wanted to do that ever since the first day we met."

"Yes, when you ran me down, you mean?" I asked, blushing.

"How else was I to get your attention?" He laughed and kissed me again.

"Where is this coming from, Michael?" I replied in shock.

"I'm crazy about you, Annie. You must have known that," he said.

The curtains opened and the audience began to applaud. Our principal, Mr. Swanson, gave an introductory speech welcoming all the parents and friends of the graduating class. The last thing I heard him say was "May I present our Valedictorian this year, Miss. . . I froze in my footsteps.

"Go on, Annie, that's you," Michael said, as he pushed me out from behind the curtains.

As I was giving my speech, I looked around the auditorium and saw only Aunt Bess. My eyes began to fill with tears. Where were they? They had promised to come. Aunt Bess had even sent them money for the bus trip. Papa had said how proud he was of my getting the highest honor. Where was he? The thought crossed my mind of the money I had been sending home and the fact that he had finally come to grips with Aunt Bess's charity, as he called it. He had found a job, not in Weston, but cleaning out stables for the neighbors. It was hard work, and he was not able to make enough money to keep the family going. Momma had taken a few jobs here and there, cleaning houses and doing ironing. Speaking of Momma, when I had written her about my graduation, she said she would not miss it for the world. Where was she? Where were my brothers and sisters?

I managed to finish my speech. The audience stood up and applauded. After Mr. Swanson handed me my diploma and congratulated me, I walked off the stage, saddened that my family had missed this very important day. "Congratulations, Annie!" Aunt Bess greeted me.

"Thank you, but where are Momma and Papa?" I asked.

Aunt Bess lowered her head and said, "I'm afraid I have some bad news, Annie. I received a wire from the hospital in Weston just before leaving the house. Your momma is very sick and needs an operation. She's in the hospital now and will be operated on tomorrow morning."

In shock and with tears streaming down my checks, I asked, "What kind of operation?"

Seeing my distress, Aunt Bess put her arms around me and held me tight. "Annie, your momma has a malignant tumor in her breast and they have to remove it."

"She has cancer?" I asked.

"I'm afraid so. But the doctor seems optimistic that if he removes her breast, she will be fine."

"I have to go home. Now!" I shouted.

"I have already made arrangements. We will fly down to Weston first thing in the morning," Bess said.

"Fly?" I asked.

"Yes, a friend of mine has a small private airplane. He told me he would be more than happy to fly us to West Virginia. We will meet him at the airport at 6:00 a.m. tomorrow."

Although I had never before been in an airplane, the fear

of flying seemed minuscule in comparison to the fear I was feeling over my mother's condition.

Last night I had the exact same dream as I had when I first arrived in Buffalo, the dream (or nightmare) where my family is floating on a raft out in the ocean. Again, I failed to get to them before a huge wave overtook their tiny raft. I could not help them. I continued to have that feeling that day, as we flew into Weston—a desperately helpless feeling.

Before I realized, we were landing at the Weston airfield. Remarkably, it took only one-third the time to fly as opposed to traveling by bus. Aunt Bess's pilot friend had arranged for her to rent a car at the airport. Noticing I had been so solemn during the flight and in the car, Aunt Bess put her arm around me and said reassuringly, "Your momma is pretty tough, she'll get through this. I'm certain of it."

"I should have stayed home with her. Maybe I could have helped." I fell against Aunt Bess's shoulder and cried all the way to the hospital.

"We're here, Annie. Now, pull yourself together," Aunt Bess said. "You need to be strong for your momma and the rest of your family."

As we rushed through the hospital's main corridor, we saw Papa and all the children sitting in the waiting room. "Has she gone into surgery yet, John?" Aunt Bess asked.

I hugged Papa and saw tears in his eyes. My brothers and sisters ran toward me and I embraced them all.

"No, not yet." he answered. "They sent us out of her room to get her ready and said they'd call us before they take her to the operating room."

"Oh, thank God! We will get to see her, Annie," Aunt Bess said in relief.

"How'd ya get here so fast?" Roy asked.

"We flew," I replied.

"Flew - in an airplane?" Frank asked.

"Yes, of course in an airplane, stupid, what else? Do you think they sprouted wings?" Roy said sarcastically.

"Stop it, both of you!" Papa said. Just then, a nurse came

down the stairs, waved Papa over, and spoke to him. Then he turned and called to us. "We can go up now, but we can't stay long."

We all ran up the stairs and into Momma's room. "Annie, Bess, you came!" I rushed to Momma's bedside and leaned over to give her a hug and a kiss. "I'm so glad to see you, my sweet Annie."

The rest of the clan gave her hugs and kisses and then Papa bent over and gently kissed her. "I love you, Kate."

"I love you too, John. I love all my family more than anything in this world. I want you all to promise me to be good to one another." There was such sadness in Momma's voice and it seemed as if she were filled with guilt and remorse.

"Kate, don't talk like that. You're going to be just fine," Aunt Bess said, almost angrily.

"Annie, Bess, come here closer, please. Annie, I want you to promise me that no matter what happens you will stay with Bess in Buffalo. I want you to continue your education and create a better life for yourself."

"But Momma. . .," I started to say.

"Please promise me. I don't want you to spend the rest of your life in these hills. Promise me!" she pleaded.

I could not refuse her plea. "Yes, Momma, I promise."

Two nurses came into the room and proceeded to wheel Momma's bed out of the room and down the hall. One of them said, "Y'all can go to the waiting room downstairs and we'll come get ya when the operation is over."

Minutes seemed like hours and the hours seemed like days. Trying to occupy the children's minds, I told them stories of Buffalo. "The street in front of Aunt Bess's house is lined with motor cars every morning and the sidewalk is filled with tons of people, all rushing to work. Downtown, a few blocks away from Aunt Bess's business, is a *whole* building that is just for artistic things, like pictures and statues. It is called the Albright Art Gallery. Alongside the city runs the biggest *creek* I've ever seen—it's called Lake Erie. Its waterfront is at the foot of Main Street, just a few blocks from our house. The lake stretches on for miles, and has all kinds of boats that navigate to and from their moorings. On this lake, there are sailboats, ocean liners, and even fishing boats. There are also tugboats that help pull larger ships into dock. They say in the wintertime the lake freezes over and the tugs still plow through the frozen harbor. At night, from my bedroom window, I can see the moon shining across the lake. It looks like millions of tiny diamonds on the water."

The children were mesmerized by my stories and started chattering amongst themselves. I glanced over and saw Papa bent over with his elbows on his knees and his face in his hands. I went over and sat down beside him. "Papa, don't worry. Momma will be alright."

"I hope so, honey; she jes' has to be. I couldn't go on if she doesn't make it through this," Papa said with tears again filling his eyes.

It had been four long hours before the doctor came out to talk with us. "John, Kate is out of surgery now."

"Thank God!" Papa interrupted. "Can we see her?"

"Nurse Johnson, would you please take the children to the cafeteria and get them something to eat?" Doctor Mead requested. "I need to talk with John and Bess alone for a minute."

"I'm staying here," I blurted out.

"Yes, Annie can stay. What is it, Doc?" Papa asked.

"I don't know how to tell you this. . ." he began.

"Tell me what? For Christ's sake, what's wrong?" Papa was yelling now. His voice was filled with fear. Only in his current state of mind would he take the Lord's name in vain.

"When we opened Kate up, we found her whole body was filled with cancer. We removed her breast but I am afraid that will not be enough. She has stage-four cancer in almost every major organ of her body."

"Oh, my God!" Papa nearly fell to the floor, weeping hopelessly.

"We can keep her in the hospital for awhile and try to make her comfortable, but it will be expensive," Dr. Mead said.

"The expense be damned!" Aunt Bess shouted with tears streaming down her face. "I'll pay for everything. Can't you do anything for my sister?"

"The only thing we can do is give her medication for the pain, but I'm afraid she doesn't have very long," he answered.

"What do you mean by very long?" Aunt Bess asked.

"I can't be sure exactly, but we're probably looking at only weeks or even days. If she only would have had this operation sooner, we might have been able to catch it in time."

"You mean she knew about this, Dr. Mead?" Bess asked.

"Yes, she's known for months," he answered. "She didn't tell any of you?"

Papa now spoke in an angry tone. "Just like her. I have been laid off for months. She probably didn't want to add to our worries."

A nurse rushed into the waiting room. "Dr. Mead, come quick. It's Kate; we think she's gone into a coma!"

Papa followed quickly behind Dr. Mead as they raced up the staircase. Aunt Bess turned to me and said, "Go ahead, Annie, I'll get the other children." I followed Papa and Dr. Mead to Momma's room. Nurses were bustling around Momma's bed, checking monitors and hooking up more tubes. Dr. Mead checked Momma's vitals and turned to Papa. "I'm afraid she has entered into a comatose state, but I don't know how long it will last."

"Is my Kate in any pain?" Papa asked.

"Probably not. This may have been her brain's way of coping with the pain," he replied.

Papa threw himself down beside Momma and said, "You can't leave me, Kate! You just can't leave me!" He was crying harder than I had ever seen him cry. It was a cry of desperation. Momma had always been the strong one in the family. She had been the leader, the one who had made all the major decisions. She was our family's matriarch. How was this family to survive without her?

"Come on John, I don't think she can hear you, and, besides, there's nothing you can do for her," Dr. Mead pleaded.

Papa would not let go of Momma. He was shaking her and telling her to wake up. "I'm not leaving her! I can't go home without her!"

"You can stay, John, but I can't let you continue shaking her like that. I will allow you to sit next to her bedside for as long as you like, but I'm sending these children home with Bess," Dr. Mead said in frustration.

Papa finally calmed down and said in a quivering voice, "Yes, Annie, have your aunt take you and the other children home. I'll stay with your momma."

Just then, Aunt Bess came into the room. "I'll take the children home, John, but I think you should come too. You need your rest."

"NO! I'm staying here with Kate!" Papa shouted and then soon calmed down again when he saw the rest of his children coming into the room. "Go with your Aunt Bess. I'll see y'all tomorrow."

"Papa, why are Momma's eyes shut?" Sarah asked.

"She's just sleeping, my little one, she's very tired. Now go home with your aunt."

On the ride home, in the car Aunt Bess had rented at the airport, the children asked a million questions. "What's wrong with Momma?" "Why is she sleeping in the middle of the day?" "When will she come home?" Most of the questions were from the youngest ones; the older children stayed very quiet.

"I'll answer all your questions when we get home," Aunt Bess said tolerantly.

Chapter 8

The following seven days were mostly spent at the hospital. Momma had not yet regained consciousness and Papa's health was beginning to deteriorate due to a lack of sleep and his refusal to eat. He had determined that if he stayed at Momma's side and talked to her, she would wake and all would be well with his world again. The younger children were confused, but the older ones were in fear of what was happening to their beloved Momma. As for me, I was numb. I had seen Uncle Charlie die and I saw the same gray coldness overcome Momma. I knew she was dying. I silently cried myself to sleep each and every night. Yet I tried to be strong and hopeful during the days that Momma was in the hospital, for the sake of the children.

I awoke early on the eighth morning to the sound of lightning cracking and thunder rumbling. I suddenly felt a cold chill run down my spine. I started to cry in rhythm to the raindrops pounding on the rooftop. Not wanting to wake the other children, I slipped downstairs to our kitchen. I brewed some coffee and sat at Gramma's oak table, recounting the dream that had awoken me so abruptly during the night, the same kind of dream I had dreamed twice before. Except this time, there were eight sharks circling the raft my family was drifting on in the ocean. Goose flesh appeared on my arms. My dear Lord, this is the eighth day Momma's been in a coma. I rushed to the living room where Aunt Bess was sleeping on the couch. "Aunt Bess, wake up. We have to get to the hospital right away!"

"My goodness, Annie, what time is it?" she asked, wiping the sleep from her eyes.

"I don't know. I just know we have to go to the hospital now! Please hurry!" I said.

We reached the hospital an hour later. Aunt Bess, the half-asleep children, and I climbed the staircase to Momma's room only to find Papa sitting in the chair by Momma's bed staring into space. Momma's bed was empty.

"Papa, where's Momma?" I asked. He did not answer. He just stared into space as if in a stupor. Hearing the commotion, Dr. Mead rushed into the room.

"I'm sorry, Annie. . . your momma. . . is gone." I felt as if my heart had been ripped from my body. Even though I knew this moment was coming, I could not speak. I could not even breathe. Momma was our world—our whole world. How could she really be gone?

"Where did she go?" Frank asked innocently.

"She went to heaven to be with God," Aunt Bess answered, trying desperately to hold back her emotions. She loved her sister deeply, but she must be strong for this family.

"Bess, I moved your sister downstairs, if you and the children want to say goodbye."

"Yes, we would. Thank you, Dr. Mead."

Dr. Mead and the nurses had moved Momma's body into a cheery room that they had filled with flowers and light. They had removed all the tubes and wires that had connected Momma to those menacing machines, and then tucked her into the covers as if she were asleep. She looked so peaceful and serene. *Finally*, I thought to myself, *she is free of pain, free of worry, and, most of all, free of the grief this world had given her*.

Aunt Bess said, "See children, your momma is sleeping with the angels now."

"I don't see no angels, Annie," Sarah said to me.

"We can't see them, but they are surely there. They are all

around her, waiting to take her to heaven to see God. Give her a kiss goodbye."

One by one, each of the children kissed Momma's cheek and said, "Goodbye, Momma." After Aunt Bess escorted all of them out of Momma's room, I knelt beside her bed and said a prayer. "Forgive me, Momma, for not being home when you needed me the most. Forgive me for not being a more grateful daughter to you and Papa. Forgive me for not being a more tolerant sister to my siblings. Forgive me, as well, for not keeping the promise I made to you, but I do promise I will take care of my brothers and sisters for as long as I live."

And so it was that a week after Momma's funeral, Aunt Bess went back to Buffalo and I stayed in West Virginia with Papa and the rest of my family. I knew this was where I belonged. In fact, this is where I should have been all along! Someone needed to take care of this family and Papa was not in any shape to deal with the responsibility. Besides, I was now sixteen and by our "hill-country" standards, I was a grown woman, and certainly capable of taking care of my family. Papa had lost all interest in finding a better job. He continued cleaning barns and doing odd jobs, but at the end of his workday, he would head for Orville's to drown his sorrow in moonshine.

I knew Papa missed Momma terribly, but I could not get him to talk about her. In fact, he would not talk about anything. When he came home from Orville's late at night he would be falling down drunk and I could hear him crying to himself out on the porch. He would then fall asleep on the sofa. In the morning, he was up and out of the house before anyone awoke. Although he never came home for dinner, I always kept leftovers for him in the icebox. Very rarely did I even see him eat. All he did was work, drink, sleep and cry. Aunt Bess and I kept in touch through letters we wrote to one another. I tried precariously not to indicate the dire situation our family was in, but sometimes I would ask her to send money. I knew she could afford it and that she was eager to help.

Surprisingly, Papa came home early one afternoon just as

the mailman deposited a letter from Aunt Bess in our mailbox. Papa opened the letter and found in it a check from our dear aunt. He was furious. He came into the house in a rage, throwing things about and yelling. "We're not a charity case! I bring in the money for this family by shoveling manure all day long. I don't need help from Bess. Annie, I want you send this back to her immediately!"

For the first time in my life, I screamed back at him. "I *will not* send it back, Papa. We need it to buy food and clothes for your children. You don't bring in enough money to go around." The despondent look on Papa's face made me want to take back what I had said, but it was too late.

As he stormed out our front door, I heard him say, "I've failed you again, Kate."

The following day, I reluctantly sent the money back and told Aunt Bess that Papa would not allow us to accept charity.

This time Papa was gone for three whole days. When he came back, he looked as if he had been on a binge for a year or more. I tried to apologize and tell him everything would work out, but he would not speak to me. Months passed by without a single word from him. I was now concerned with his health, for he looked like death warmed over.

During the daytime, I took over Momma's job, cleaning houses and taking in laundry. At night, I went to work at our local school once the children were fed and tucked safely into bed. I scrubbed and cleaned all the classrooms at the school to help make ends meet. Several times, Jamey and James asked if they could quit school and find a job to help with money, but I refused to consider it.

The holidays were nearing and I began to worry how I could make them as meaningful and joyous as Momma had always done. I could not even talk to Papa about how we would manage Christmas, for it had now become his habit to disappear for days on end. The sadness of losing his beloved wife had become all-consuming and had alienated him from his children.

Just a week before Christmas, the school had told me they

could no longer pay me for my cleaning services. Evidently, the whole county had slipped into the depths of the depression. The mill had shut down and families were moving to distant towns in hopes of finding jobs and a better life. Stores in Weston were closing due to the lack of customers. Roy had lost his job in Weston. Desperate times created desperate situations. Not only were we caught up in a financial disaster, but this winter had become exceptionally harsh. It seemed as if the snow would never stop falling, with over several feet being dumped on our little piece of the earth. Everything stopped! Roads were closed. Schools were closed. Even our mail delivery came to a screeching halt.

I had depleted the root cellar of all the canned goods Momma had put up two summers ago. This past summer she had become too ill to do any canning at all or even harvest the vegetables from our garden. I was at least thankful that we had flour to make bread and a few chickens that were still laying eggs. Today, however, I had to kill a chicken so that we would have something to eat for supper. It was my first time, and I detested the task. Papa had always performed this dastardly deed. Unfortunately, for me, he had not been around for several days, so I had to take it upon myself. After the execution of this poor chicken, I could only relish in the thought that we would eat well tonight! As I sat plucking the feathers from this poor innocent bird, thoughts of all the culinary delights I had enjoyed at Aunt Bess's home came rushing through my mind.

Because of the inclement weather over the past few weeks, contact with Aunt Bess had been completely suspended. Her letters of encouragement and hope had been a sustaining factor in my day-to-day performance of running this family. On occasion, she would plead with me to bring the family to Buffalo to live with her, but I explained Papa would never dream of it and I certainly could not leave him behind. Speaking of Papa, where had he been all this time? Why was he not here sharing my dismay over our family's situation? Maybe, I thought, he couldn't get home because of the snow. As if I didn't have enough to worry about, now I was consumed with worry of his welfare. At least he would be proud of my abstention from dreaming of sailing the seven seas. My daydreams had most certainly not been filled with such foolishness, but instead were filled with thoughts of food (or should I say, the lack of it). I had become a bit emaciated. My clothes hung on my lithesome body because I had done without, in lieu of my siblings' insatiable appetites.

The longer Papa was away, the angrier I became with him. How could he abandon us? How could he leave us to fend for ourselves? Where in the world was he? Had he been hurt? Was he sick? Was he even alive? Or, was he just stinkin' drunk? My questions would soon be answered.

Christmas Eve came far too quickly. I had taken some of the clothes Uncle Charlie and Aunt Bess had bought for me and altered them for new outfits that Janey, Lizzy, and Sarah could wear. With the leftover scraps, I made caps and scarves for Roy, James, and Frank. For baby Jacob I polished up the windpipe Papa had made for me a few years back. I spent every night, after the children were in bed, sewing with thread and needle until my fingers bled. This Christmas Eve, I decided to bake cookies (although a wasteful use of my flour and sugar supply) so the children would have a sweet treat when they awoke on Christmas morning. Finally finished with the presents and the cookies, I dragged my tired and aching body to bed. No sooner did I start drifting off to dreamland, when I was awakened by a loud, booming sound. It almost sounded like a crack of thunder, but that was unlikely since it was December. Out of curiosity, I climbed out of my warm bed and trudged downstairs. Oddly enough, the kitchen light was on and I was sure I had turned it out when I had gone to bed. When I started to turn it off again, I noticed a letter on the table.

"Dear Annie" it began. "I don't know what else to do. I loved your momma more than life itself. I failed her and now I have failed you. Please tell the children I love them. My Christmas present to you and the other children is a $500 life insurance policy your Momma had bought years ago. It is all I have to give you. I'm sorry I haven't been here and that I left you with all the responsibilities. I just couldn't look into your faces without seeing your momma. It hurt too much. Please don't hate me. Love, your papa." Under the letter from Papa lay his insurance policy, neatly folded.

I sat at the table, stunned. "No, Papa! No!" I cried. I suddenly remembered the sound that had awakened me. "Oh, my God!" I rushed to the front door and could see a lantern light hanging in the barn. I flew outside with just my nightgown on and headed for the barn. I couldn't even feel the freezing cold of the snow that I had plummeted into; I just plowed through the depths of it, to the barn. When I reached the closed door, I froze in my tracks. I must have been there at least five minutes before I felt a hand on my shoulder.

"Open it, Annie," Roy said. "I read the letter. Open the door."

"I can't," I said.

Although Roy was only fourteen, he seemed wise beyond his years at this moment. I looked at him with fear in my eyes. "Why did he do this?" Roy said nothing. He opened the barn door and we saw Papa laying face down on the hay-covered floor with blood gushing from his head. "Oh my God, Papa!" Roy took me in his arms and tried to comfort me. I was shaking violently and crying uncontrollably.

"Go back to the house and make sure none of the kids woke up. I'll take care of this."

"What are we going to do?" I asked.

"I'm going to cover him up and then I'll walk to Orville's house to get help."

"You can't walk to Orville's in this snow!"

"I'll be fine. Just go back to the house before you catch your death of cold."

I was astonished with Roy's mature demeanor. When did this little boy become a man? I was utterly amazed with the way he took charge of the situation, but also thankful, for I had become a sobbing excuse for a woman, unable to control my emotions. As I left the barn, I turned to watch Roy cover Papa with a horse blanket. “This will keep you warm, Papa,” Roy silently whispered. My heart broke!

I managed to reach the house without falling down in the snow. Luckily, no other children had awoken. I sat at the table shivering and crying for what seemed like hours until I heard men talking to each other, out in the barn. Just as I opened our front door, Roy came in. “Mr. Thompson and Mr. Means were at Orville’s so they came too,” he told me. “They said they would take Papa to the coroner in Weston tonight. Mr. Means said he would send his wife up day after tomorrow to stay with the kids, while we go to the funeral parlor. I told them thank you and that I would check on you and the kids.”

“Roy, thank you for being so grown up. I just couldn’t handle this,” I said as I hugged him.

“You’ve had to deal with a lot these past few months, Annie. It’s time I stepped up and helped. Did any of the kids wake up?”

“No, thank God!” I answered. “What are we going to tell them?”

“This probably sounds terrible, but do you think we can wait until the day after Christmas to tell them?” Roy asked.

“No, Roy it doesn’t sound terrible. It’s the right thing to do. Papa wouldn’t have wanted to ruin their Christmas,” I answered.

It was almost daylight so I made a pot of strong black coffee for Roy and me as we awaited the first sounds of little footsteps on the staircase. This was not going to be an easy day. For the children’s sake, we had to act as if nothing were wrong. Roy and I talked about the insurance policy and said we must not show anyone the note that Papa had left. In order to collect the insurance money, Papa’s death had to appear an accident. In fact, as far as the children, we decided to tell them he had an accident. No one needed to know that Papa had taken his own life. Roy and I would share this secret to our dying day. We would say that Papa was just cleaning his rifle when it accidentally discharged.

Christmas was pleasant, at least for the children. Roy and I became very close that day and have remained so ever since. Throughout that Christmas day, Roy would put his arm around my shoulders to comfort me when I was feeling close to crying. I remember several of the children asking where Papa was.

"Papa loves Christmas. Why isn't he here?" Lizzy asked. My insides quivered, not knowing how to answer her.

Christmas Day had finally ended. All the children were tucked away in their beds, while Roy and I stayed up most of the night deciding how to tell them about Papa. We would sit them all down at the table and tell them that Papa had an accident and that now he was with Momma in heaven to keep her company. We also decided to send a wire to Aunt Bess, asking her to come. I told Roy that, on several occasions, Aunt Bess had invited us to come live with her in Buffalo, but I wasn't sure I wanted to burden her with eight extra mouths to feed.

"She's rich, ain't she?" Roy asked.

"Well, yes but. . ." I started to reply, and then Roy interrupted.

"Where else can we go? What else can we do?"

"You're right. We'll talk more about it when she gets here," I replied.

Morning came all too soon and the task of telling the children about Papa was upon us. With the exception of Janey and James, the children believed our little white lie. We cried together and held each other as tight as we could. Losing both parents in the short span of only a few months was devastating. As for Janey and James, we could tell they knew something was awry but they never uttered a word of disbelief. Thank goodness!

"Oh my dear Lord!" Aunt Bess exclaimed, as she read the wire Roy and I had sent her. "How could this happen to these poor children?"

"What's the matter?" Maria asked.

"My brother-in-law is dead! Kate's husband. Annie's dad.

The wire says he accidentally shot himself while cleaning his rifle."

"Oh no, how terrible!" Maria said, as she bowed her head and blessed herself.

"Annie writes that it happened on Christmas Eve. Those poor children, losing both of their parents. That's it! I must go to them immediately and they're coming back to live with me. Maria, please have Russell bring the car around to the front."

"Yes, of course," Maria said dutifully.

As Aunt Bess scurried around getting her suitcase packed, she passed the bedroom her niece had occupied for such a short time. She went in and sat on the edge of the bed. "My poor Annie, what you've gone through this past year is too much for anyone to bear. I won't take any excuses for not coming back here with me." She then blessed herself and prayed. "Kate, my beloved sister, I will take good care of your family. I promise you they will get a proper education and have a good life here with me. And Kate, I will make sure they will never forget what a wonderful mother and father they all had."

"Bess, the car is waiting for you out front," Maria called to her.

"Maria, please call my office and tell them I will be in West Virginia for a few days. Could you also get the spare bedrooms ready, please? I'll be bringing eight children back with me."

"You'll be bringing how many back?" Maria asked in shock.

"Eight beautiful nieces and nephews," Bess replied with a smile. She had always wanted a large family. Now, by the fate of God, she would have them.

"Take me to the airport, Russell. I'm going to fly to West Virginia."

Chapter 9

Five Years Later

As I sat on the dock where the *Annie* is moored, I found myself staring out at my imposing Lake Erie. Its powerful waves splash against her hull, rocking her back and forth arduously. I watched the sun as it descended into the water like a ball of fire, almost sizzling from the coldness of the water. Just before it disappeared completely into the depths of the lake, its golden light cast shimmering yellow diamonds on the water. I looked to the sky in hopes that Momma and Papa were sharing with me this delightful presentation of God's work.

For the last few years, Aunt Bess and I had been diligently working to launch the *Annie*. Our dreams had finally come to fruition. The *Annie* was launched and christened on the anniversary of Uncle Charlie's death. "A tribute to a great man," Aunt Bess had said. Although our magnificent ship had yet to sail the waters beyond, I vigilantly watched over her every spare moment of my now very busy life. Since I graduated *cum laude* from the University of Buffalo the year before, I had worked side by side with my dear aunt. She told me that I was her protégé and someday I would be successful at running her business.

Due to her love, care and generosity, all of my siblings had thrived since Aunt Bess brought us from the hills of West Virginia. Roy, now nineteen, was scheduled for college in the fall. Janey and James were in their last two years of high school. Frank, at fourteen, displayed all the hormonal awkwardness of a teenager. Lizzy, now twelve, had started to bloom into a beautiful young lady, with Sarah, now eleven, following in her footsteps. Jacob, still the baby of the family at age eight, had become a mischievous handful. Ever since Aunt Bess opened her magnanimous heart and home to my clan, I had seen them evolve from devastated, orphaned children to happy, healthy, and nurtured young people. Aunt Bess told me they had survived the tragedies of their lives because of my strong, virtuous character and because I had passionately devoted my life to their success. All I know is that, as the oldest, Momma and Papa would have expected nothing less from me.

Since moving to Buffalo, the children had developed numerous friendships and marvelous social lives. I, on the other hand, hadn't taken the time to socialize. Working all day at the office and factory, then going to school at night to complete my education, had left me with little time for myself. What time I did have left in each day was spent on helping my siblings with their schoolwork and guaranteeing their happiness. Once the children were in their beds for the evening, I would wander down to the docks to watch over the *Annie*. I often sat there and dreamed of sailing her out into Lake Erie and beyond.

One specific evening, I was feeling particularly melancholy. My daydreams now consisted of the way my life used to be as a child. I yearned to be young again. I longed for the feeling of security that my parents had provided me. I missed the smells of Momma cooking in the kitchen and the anticipation of Papa returning home after work. Most of all, I missed the warmth of watching Papa kiss Momma with the passion and love he had for her. *Would I ever find that kind of love*? I asked myself.

Fortunately, however, the sounds of the pounding waves muffled my discontented sniveling. The boisterous waves had also concealed the sounds of a visitor walking on the dock towards me. I suddenly felt a gentle hand on my shoulder.

"Do you come here every night?"

With trepidation, I turned to see that this docile voice belonged to Michael. "You scared me half to death, Michael O'Connor. What are you doing here?"

"I enjoy watching your magnificent sailboat whenever I get the chance. And you?" Michael replied.

Michael and I had developed what you might call a platonic relationship. He admittedly felt more for me than I was ready for. Ever since he kissed me at my high school graduation, I had resisted his every attempt for something more. Although he had grown into quite a handsome young man, my responsibilities relating to my family had deterred me from pursuing such romantic nonsense. In fact, Michael's looks had become the topic of all the female workers at the office. His curly brown hair framed a perfectly shaped face. Long dark lashes accented his deep green eyes, and his finely chiseled jaw conferred the strength that accompanied his immensely masculine stature.

"I come here to think," I said.

Michael gently took my face in his hands. "Looks to me like you've been crying."

I wiped the tears from my eyes and embarrassingly responded, "Nonsense!"

"Annie, you don't have to be strong in front of me. What's wrong?"

"Michael, you know me too well. . . I guess I just miss the old days. I miss Momma and Papa and the way my life used to be," I said.

He swiftly lifted me into his arms and hugged me long and hard. "You've been through so much in your life. You're entitled to be sad once in awhile." He then kissed my cheek tenderly and said, "Come on, I'm going to take you to the ice cream parlor. What you need is a big, fat, chocolate sundae!"

"For the life of me, Michael, I will never understand why you care for a silly girl like me. You do know that every single girl at my office would die to have you even say hello to her. I swear they're all madly in love with you."

"Maybe so, but you're the one I want," he said smiling.

"But why?" I asked. "I'm extremely plain and much too skinny!"

"That's why I want to take you for ice cream. . . to fatten you up a little bit. Besides, I am completely captivated by your intelligence and charm," he replied.

"You are absolutely incorrigible, Michael O'Connor!" I said. "Come on; let's get a double-decker, hot-fudge sundae with whipped cream and nuts."

"Hey, don't forget the cherry on top!" Michael said.

As always, Michael had rescued me from my despair and we spent the next hour eating ice cream, talking, and laughing. Michael attended the University of Buffalo just as I had, and always talked of becoming a doctor. I had assumed that now we both were graduated, he would go on to medical school. However, this evening he told me he was planning to enlist in the Navy.

"You can't be serious, Michael," I said.

"Why? What do you mean? I think serving my country is a noble thing to do," Michael retorted.

"Well, do you know there's a war going on in Europe and in Asia?" I asked.

"Yes, I know, but. . ."

"Do you also know that the fascist nations of Germany, Italy and Japan are attempting to conquer the free world?" I asked.

"I know all about that, but what if they want to conquer our country? Don't you want me to defend helpless citizens like you?" he asked. "Besides, if I don't enlist, I could be drafted eventually, anyway!"

"Not if you're in college, Michael!" I said.

"I'm done with school," he stated sharply. "Besides, my father went to the first war when he was my age. I'm sure he expects me to fulfill my duty to my country, as well."

"Have you talked with him about it?" I asked.

"Not yet, but it won't make any difference. I'm going, and that's that!"

"Oh Michael, don't be foolish! You could be injured or even killed."

"So you do care about me?" he asked with a smile.

"Of course I care about you. You're my dearest friend!" I replied.

Not hearing the answer he wanted, Michael said, "Let's change the subject. You're getting upset again."

We finished our sundaes and Michael walked me home. We promised not to speak of his going into the Navy again that night, but I knew somehow, some way, I would have to talk him out of it. After all, there was no way I was going to lose another person that I loved. Not again! Suddenly a flush of emotion surged through my body. Did I just say "love"? When he escorted me to my front door, I reached up and kissed him square on the lips. He abruptly backed away.

Michael then breathlessly whispered my name—"Annie"—, and pulled me back towards him, gently pressed his body against mine. His head titled slightly, as his warm lips softly caressed my own. His hand slid to the small of my back and guided me even closer to him, as he kissed me deeper and deeper. My lips were eager and on fire and my body was responding to the tenderness of his touch.

"Oh Michael, you just can't go away!" I whispered in his ear.

Unexpectedly, he again backed away from our embrace. "Is this just a ploy to keep me from enlisting?"

"So what if it is? Is there something wrong with me not wanting you to go?" I asked.

"Jeepers, Annie! Here I thought you actually felt something for me, finally. What a fool I am!" Michael turned in disgust and started walking down the porch stairs.

"Michael, don't be so pig-headed. I do care for you. You know I do! Don't go away angry!"

"Care for me? I felt more in that kiss than just caring and I thought you felt it too. I love you, Annie! I always have and I always will and I'm not ashamed to admit it." Taking my hand in his, Michael continued, "I want to be with you for the rest of my life. When I serve my time in the Navy and return home, I want to marry you."

"Michael, you have my head swimming. I don't know what to say."

"Say you love me too," he pleaded.

"I can't," I replied, as my voice started to quiver.

"Why not?" Michael asked.

"Because. . . loving someone hurts!"

Chapter 10

Two weeks had gone by without another word from Michael about the Navy. We both knew that if we talked of it, an argument would ensue. This evening, Michael was invited to our birthday celebration for Sarah. All my brothers and sisters loved Michael. The boys respected him and viewed him as a role model, and all the girls had a crush on him because of his good looks and sense of humor. I greeted Michael at the door with a warm hug and a kiss. The rest of evening was filled with joy and laughter. Then, just before Michael was to leave, he dropped the proverbial bomb on his adoptive family.

"Tomorrow morning I will be boarding the train to go to the Naval Training Center in Great Lakes, Illinois," he announced.

Everyone's jaw dropped in astonishment. I had neglected to mention to any of them that Michael had enlisted in the Navy. This oversight was due in part to the fact that I was sure I could dissuade him from doing so.

"Michael, you can't go away!" Sarah cried.

Aunt Bess added, "Why would you go and do a fool thing like that?"

"Well, I think it's exciting!" Roy announced.

"Will you be on a big ship?" James asked.

"I don't know what they'll do with me," Michael said, "but I'm hoping to serve on an aircraft carrier eventually. Right now, though, I'll be at training camp for eight weeks."

"We'll miss you, Michael!" the girls said in unison.

"As soon as I'm assigned, I'll send you all a postcard." Hugs and kisses followed Michael out the front door.

When we reached the end of the front porch, he turned to me and said, "Will you see me off at the railroad station, Annie?"

With reluctance, I bowed my head in defeat and said, "Yes, of course. What time do you leave?"

"The train departs at 6:30 a.m., but could you come earlier? I need to talk to you about something."

"I'll be there at 6:00, OK?" I asked.

"That's great, see ya then!" Michael kissed me on the cheek before he turned to run down the steps and down the sidewalk to his home.

A cold chill ran down my spine and my heart started pounding as I watched him disappear down the street. *What could I do to make him stay? Was it too late to change his mind? What did he want to talk to me about? Would he ask me to marry him again? What would I say?*

My sleepless night had turned into morning only too quickly. I spent the entire night tossing and turning, pondering my feelings for Michael. At 5:00 a.m., I stared at my alarm clock as it redundantly chimed to wake me. The few moments I had fallen asleep during the night, I was immediately engulfed in a terrifying dream. My dream was very similar to the dreams of Momma and Papa floating on a raft in the sea. This time, however, I was the one drifting, and not on a raft, but on the *Annie*. The air was still. There was no wind for her sails. She seemed lifeless in the water. As I looked ahead, I could see that I was nearing a deep, black whirlpool in the ocean. The closer the *Annie* came to the black hole, the larger the chasm became. All of a sudden, my ship was sucked into this ominous twirling abyss. I was thrown from the helm and flew off the deck into the sky above her. She flipped over with her bottom up, and I landed on the main beam of her hull. I was hanging on for dear life as she circled the perimeter of the whirlpool with her masts plunging deeper into the vast depths of that black hole.

Tremendous fear surged through my entire body as I heard Michael's voice calling me from the bowels of the ocean. Then I awoke.

I shuddered as the recollection of my dream filled me again with fear and anxiety. Although reluctant to leave my bed, I went to the bathroom to splash cold water on my tired eyes. The pending confrontation with Michael filled my emotional being. *Would his family be at the station? Would he announce his love for me in front of them? What will I say?*

My questions were soon answered as I reached the train station and saw Michael standing solitarily at the entrance gate.

"Good morning, sunshine!" Michael smiled as he gave me a kiss on the cheek.

In my opinion, that had always been a definite flaw in his character: he was a "morning person". . . I was not.

"Morning," I replied in a disgruntled tone. "What did you want to talk to me about? I hope you're not going to ask me for my approval in this ridiculous decision of yours!"

"No, I'm not asking for your approval. I've made up my mind. This is something I have to do." His smiley demeanor abruptly turned into a seriously earnest disposition. "I've already told you how I feel about you. I love you with all my heart, Annie, and want to marry you. At this time, however, I'm not sure how you feel about me." Michael reached into his coat pocket and pulled out a small box.

Not until that very moment, with the thought of losing him filling my mind, did I realize how much I truly cared for him. My whole body began to tremble. My heart felt as if it were in my throat, choking the breath right out of me. I couldn't speak. I couldn't move. I was frightened. Frightened by what I was feeling, that fear engulfed my very soul. Loving, to me, meant pain and sadness. I had known, all too well, what loving and losing someone felt like, and the loss of a loved one is too agonizing. I didn't want to feel that way ever again. I didn't want to give in to this indomitable emotion. I had always prided myself on the fact that I could restrain my feelings and control my emotions. I had convinced myself it wasn't sensible to love anyone, because the pain from losing that love was unbearable. But right at that moment, as I looked into Michael's gentle, caring eyes, I felt powerless over what my heart was telling me. It was telling me I was in love. I was madly and passionately in love with this man standing before me. A man who had been just a "good friend" for so many years. A man who had stood by me through thick and thin, through good times and bad. A man who had loved me despite my weaknesses. A man who had survived my obstinacy and my callous nature. Yes, I do indeed love this man standing before me. . . a man who is now going to leave.

"Are you going to open it?" Michael asked after handing me the little black box.

"I. . . I. . .yes, I'm going to open it." My hands were shaking so badly I could hardly maneuver the simple clasp. "Oh, my goodness, Michael, it's beautiful!" I exclaimed as my eyes gazed upon the most magnificent heart-shaped diamond I had ever seen.

"You like it, then?" he asked.

"I love it!" I replied breathlessly.

"Do you love me?" Michael asked apprehensively

All my doubts and fears disappeared as I replied wholeheartedly, "Yes, Michael O'Connor, I do love you. I love you desperately!"

As I leaped towards him, he abruptly stopped me by holding his hands on my shoulders. "Will you marry me, Annie?"

"Yes, yes, most definitely yes!" I answered.

As we embraced, I felt an overwhelming warmth and joy, a joy that had been missing from my life for a very long time. Love—what a breathtaking emotion! Why had I been so reluctant towards this emotion? The exhilaration was remarkable. I felt as if my heart had taken wings and my soul was soaring above the clouds.

"I love you, my sweet Annie," Michael said as he lifted my face gently with his two hands and kissed me ever so softly. "I can't wait until I'm out of the Navy. As soon as I graduate from training camp, I get a two-week leave. We can be married then, before I am deployed."

Suddenly my soaring soul came crashing back to earth. The realization of my love going away hit me like a ton of bricks. "Oh, Michael, I hope you'll be stationed close to home. I can't bear the thought of you being too far away."

"I have to go where I'm needed, and that could most likely be overseas. You know that." As I started to object, the train whistle blew. "I have to go, Annie. I'll be back before you know it. I'll write to you everyday if I can. I love you."

Michael held me tight and kissed me hard. Then he was gone.

Chapter 11

October 3, 1941

It had been two weeks since Michael had departed from the Buffalo train station en route to the Great Lakes Naval Training Camp in Illinois. Even though I had been patiently waiting on my front porch steps every day, nothing had arrived, not even a postcard. That day, while I sat awaiting the postman, I could feel the cool gentle breeze from the Lake as it rustled through the trees along the sidewalk. I normally loved this time of year with its crimson colors and crisp refreshing winds, but the longing to hear from Michael had my senses disconcerted. If only I could receive a postcard or *something,* then perhaps my life could return to normal.

In an attempt to focus elsewhere, I thought to myself, *What a great day for sailing,* but the lake looks rough and a bit rowdy. Regrettably, I hadn't been on the *Annie* in quite some time. In the evenings, though, I still managed to sit on the docks and watch her dance with the water. Joseph from work had rounded up a crew for the *Annie* a few years after Uncle Charlie had passed away, but we had only taken her out a few times. The business (Aunt Bess's business) of constructing homes and ships can be ever so time consuming. That, along with looking after my siblings—who were now becoming very independent and trying of my patience—had become a full time career.

"Hello there, Miss Annie," the postman called out from a half a block down the street.

"Hi, Andy," I replied.

We were now on a first-name basis since I began frequenting these ole porch steps. Each day that he arrived with the mail, he quickly leafed through his pouch in search of what I had been awaiting. He saw the anticipation on my eager face and was saddened when nothing turned up from Michael. The day before, he told me that Mr. and Mrs. O'Connor hadn't received any mail from Mikey either. That's what he called Michael. "I've known that boy ever since he was knee high to a grasshopper." He smiled with a broad grin. "I just know he'll write to ya soon. The first few weeks I was in the Army, they kept me so busy and worked me so hard; I didn't have the time or the energy to write home."

That day, however, he had an uncommon gait as he approached our house. He was actually skipping and whistling. "You seem extraordinarily cheerful today, Andy." At the end of our sidewalk, he unexpectedly came to a halt, and from behind his back, he presented a long, white envelope, waving it back and forth in the air.

"Guess what I have here, Miss Annie?"

Knowing exactly what he did have, I ran towards him at breakneck speed, nearly running him over. "Please don't tease me," I begged him.

"See, I told you Mikey would write ya once he got settled in," he said with a smile as broad as Texas.

"Thank you, thank you, and thank you!" I said as I ripped the letter from his hand and gave him a kiss on the cheek.

"Wow, this job ain't half bad after all! I'll probably be seein' ya 'bout every day now; with either one comin' in, or one goin' out."

As I waved to him, I ran into the house screaming that I had received a letter from Michael. Everyone came running into Uncle Charlie's den (or reading room, as I called it). After a few moments of just staring at his handwriting, I began:

Dearest Annie,

We arrived at camp at 12:30 p.m. on the 30th and went straight to initiation to check in. Then we stood in line for hours, getting haircuts and being examined by the doctors. After that, we were all assigned to our barracks. This place is huge. They have three camps in the training facility: Camp Dewey, Camp Downs, and Camp Porter. Each camp consists of a group of barracks, drill fields, obstacle courses, showers, heads (those are the bathrooms), and the mess hall (that's where we eat).I was assigned to Camp Dewey, which seems to be the largest of them all. There are bunk beds from one end of my barracks to the other, and I share a bunk with Tommy, who happens to be from Fink, West Virginia. Have you ever heard of Fink? I told him my *fiancée* was from West Virginia (or West-By-God-Virginia, as he called it). Anyway, he has that same southern accent you have. So far, we get along great!

They have us marching for hours on end, and then today we had a rifle drill while we marched. I have blisters on my feet as big as half-dollars. After marching, we have to go through the obstacle courses and calisthenics. Good thing I'm in shape. Some of the guys here are having an awful time because they're overweight. By the end of the day, I'm so tired I can hardly eat. I'm starting to get used to it now, so hopefully I can start writing to you every day (or at least every other day.)

Everyone here is talking about the Germans' brutal bombing attacks on London and the sinking of the British ship, the *Hood*. Then the Nazis went on to attack the Soviet Union. After that, the German Gestapo started exterminating Jews and Gypsies by gassing them in camps. The stories I hear makes me sick to my stomach.

I miss you terribly, Annie. As soon as each day ends and I hit the sack, I start dreaming of you and back home. I love you so much it hurts.

Well, they just called for "lights out." I'll get this in the mailbag first thing in the morning. Write to me soon.

Love, Michael

As soon as I started reading the last part of Michael's letter, the boys left saying, "Oh no this is the 'mushy part'." However, my sisters sat even closer, chanting, "Oh, he's so romantic!"

After reading Michael's letter, I began to recall the newspapers reporting on how once the Japanese occupied southern Indochina, President Roosevelt froze Japanese assets in the United States. They suspended relations with Japan, and announced an oil embargo against all aggressor states, including Germany. With the aggression overseas continuing, I began to fear that Michael would soon be caught up in a full-scale war between the United States and Germany.

One good thing about the war: Buffalo was again flourishing. Jobs were abundant and the city was growing by leaps and bounds. The P-40 Warhawk fighter planes that were manufactured in Tonawanda (just outside of Buffalo) were being exported to North Africa for the British Air Force. With over five million dollars in war supply contracts, Buffalo began to do more war business with the federal government than all but four other cities in the country.

The eight-week stint of Michael's training in the Great Lakes was all but over, filling me with enormous anticipation. We had written back and forth to each other on a daily basis he, telling of his hardships as a boot-camp trainee, and I, telling of my hardships as a future bride with all the preparation for our upcoming wedding. I had once suggested a small, intimate wedding with just family, but Aunt Bess would hear nothing of the sort. "My dear, we have so many friends and co-workers who would be deeply offended if not invited to the biggest event of the decade. Besides, with all your brothers and sisters making up the wedding party itself, there would be no one to fill the seats in the church."

So it came to be that our wedding was to become Buffalo's main event for the year! When the guest list was finally complete, over 150 people were invited. I began to see the cost of this affair as being prohibitive, and of course, the wedding party had to be dressed in the finest attire that money could buy. Each time I would raise the subject of money, Aunt Bess would scowl at me and say, "The business is doing very well because of the war. Besides, your Uncle Charlie would have wanted you to have the finest. I just wish he and your momma and papa could be here to see it."

The day came when we all had to be fitted for our wedding attire. Still being that poor "country bumpkin" down deep inside, I told Aunt Bess that all I wanted was a very simple wedding dress. *What was I thinking?* Of course, according to my aunt, I had to have "the designer dress" of the century. When I went into the dress shop, I was amazed to see four seamstresses, two millineries, and three shoemakers waiting to dote on me hand and foot (literally).

I never realized in my wildest dreams that creating such an affair was so demanding and time consuming. In fact, for the past few weeks I had done nothing but prepare for this event, *my wedding*! I hadn't been working at the office because Aunt Bess insisted that I spend time on the wedding instead of behind my desk. I hadn't even spent much time with my family. What annoyed me as well was that I hadn't had the time to just sit and watch the *Annie*. The crew, which now included Roy, James, Janey, and Frank who had become quite accomplished sailors—had taken the *Annie* out only twice since the beginning of the fall season. Given the history of Buffalo winters, there would be only one or two more chances for sailing before she was put in dry dock. However, with the wedding plans proceeding and Michael's homecoming on December 5, chances of sailing again that year seemed impossible.

One of my letters to Michael offered a solution to all this wedding madness. "We should run away to get married and then sail the *Annie* all around the Great Lakes for our honeymoon," I had told him.

He wrote back in reply, "Annie, you know that would break your family's heart. Right now, though, I wish I could go AWOL and come running home to you and into your loving arms. I miss you so much my heart aches. I miss the smell of your hair. I miss the softness of your skin. I miss the sweetness of your lips. I miss the way your body feels against mine when I hold you near. I can't wait to make you my wife."

Feeling a warm flush all over my body, I swiftly tucked this particular letter under my pillow, knowing I couldn't dare show the rest of my family Michael's deepest feelings. I remember saying, after being asked to read the letter, "Oh, it's just more about boot camp; nothing at all you'd be interested in hearing."

As the time of Michael's return was approaching, newspapers were filled with updates on the war. Germany's Nazi troops continued to tramp through Europe. The world's emerging perception that Hitler was becoming the butcher of humanity escalated their fear of war. The Japanese-United States relationship became increasingly strained as Japan moved toward greater power in the Pacific. Japanese troop transports flowed steadily southward. The Japanese demanded U.S. aid to China be stopped but the U.S. refused to do so. However, Tokyo sent their representative, Kurusu, to Washington with a new formula for peaceful settlement. On November 27, Kurusu met with President Roosevelt, but by December 3, talks had reached an impasse. The Japanese were not ready to give up negotiations and reiterated their desire for peace.

They made a new appointment with Secretary Hull for December 7, 1941.

Chapter 12

On December 5, 1941 at 3:45 p.m., Michael's train from the Great Lakes rolled into the Buffalo station. I was standing as close to the gate as possible when the train's whistle blew and steam escaped from her engine. At first, all I could see were clouds of steam that permeated the air and blurred figures that were exiting the train cars. Then I saw this tall, handsome sailor, dressed in his winter blues, advance towards me. My heart skipped a beat as I called out, "Michael?"

"Annie!" the handsome sailor replied.

No other words were spoken for several blissful moments. We just stood there, face to face, with pure ecstasy in our hearts. Then, with irrepressible passion, we embraced and kissed each other for what seemed like an eternity, while I was thinking that *an eternity was not long enough*! Although all I wanted was to stay in his strong, muscular arms and look into his emerald green eyes, I swiftly scuttled him off to our awaiting car.

"Hello, Mr. Michael, welcome home," Russell said.

"Thank you, Russell. I can't tell you how glad I am to be home," Michael said as he kissed me. "I've missed my sweet Annie so much." He then turned to Russell and asked, "Could we stop at my house, first? I want to see my parents"

"Would you mind waiting for us at Michael's?" I asked Russell.

"No, of course not, Miss Annie," he replied.

Michael and I looked at each and started to laugh. "Russell, you will have to call her 'Mrs. Annie' soon."

Russell grinned and replied, "Yessir."

After we visited with Michael's parents for a few moments, we headed for Aunt Bess's house, which by now had become the hub (or I should say the "headquarters") of wedding central. When we walked into the main foyer, the family and house staff were awaiting us. "Welcome home, Michael." They all cheered and then one by one came up to hug him or shake his hand. With the wedding only one day away, there was much to discuss with Michael, so Aunt Bess invited us both into the parlor. We talked of when we needed to go to the church and what was expected of us. Then, Aunt Bess explained that, since the wee hours of this morning, everyone in the house had been decorating, cooking, and planning the "grand" reception that was to take place here in Aunt Bess's home after the wedding ceremony.

In the middle of everyone talking, Michael leaned over and whispered in my ear, "Come with me, my sweet wife to be." Michael gently put his arm around my waist and directed me to the foyer. He then opened the door to the coat closet, and escorted me inside.

"What in the world are you doing?" I asked.

Once the closet door was closed behind us, I found myself next to Michael in a dark, two foot by two foot room, with only a breath between us. "I've been waiting for this for hours." He then pulled me towards him even closer and said, "I love you." Our eager lips came together like magnetic fields and I was sure nothing could ever part us.

"I love you, Michael, more than anything in this world," I said. I was sure that at this moment nothing would ever hurt me again, not as long as I had him by my side.

After a few more moments together, we finally rejoined the parlor occupants and their conversations. Maria rushed to Michael's side and began to show him the menu for the reception. He stopped her in her tracks and said, "Maria, you're the best cook this side of the Mississippi. Anything you prepare will be wonderful!"

Several other questions were presented to us before Aunt Bess finally said, "Alright, you two, I know you want to be alone for a while. So be gone with ya!" We excused ourselves and slipped away to the front porch. As we sat on the swing, holding each other as closely as possible, I accidentally knocked Michael sailor's cap (he called it a "Dixie cup") off his head.

"Oh, my goodness, what did they do to your beautiful curly locks? I know you said you had to get a hair cut, but you're nearly bald!" I said in dismay.

Michael started laughing, "Everyone has to get a buzz cut, because they want to make sure no one has lice or anything like that."

"Oh, that's disgusting Michael. Don't they know you come from a good home?" I said.

"It doesn't matter what they know—it's procedure. What's the matter? Don't you love me anymore now that I am bald?" Michael asked, smiling with that beautiful smile of his.

"Silly man, I'd love you even if you had a big ole wart on your nose!"

December 6, 1941 - Our Wedding Day

I awoke that morning with a knot in my stomach the size of a grapefruit. I hadn't realized that I would be so nervous; but I was not only nervous, I was down right terrified! My problems with intimacy had been a long-running quandary for me. The physicality of this whole marriage phenomenon, quite honestly, scared me to death. Up to this point in my life, Michael's passionate kisses had been the only intimacy I had ever experienced. I say that with shame, for my mother had already borne four babies by the time she was my age. As I have said before, in the hills of West Virginia, I would be considered a dried-up, prune of an old maid by now.

I struggled to my feet and went into my charming pink

bathroom to wash the sleep from my eyes. What I saw in the mirror was not a rosy-cheeked woman who was about to be married, but a pasty, chalky-faced innocent. At this moment, anxiety and fear set in and nausea rose from the core of my stomach. I was not certain I could face the upcoming festivities. *I love Michael with all my heart, but what if I'm not able to measure up to his standards as a wife?* I asked myself. I stood frozen in front of that mirror, unable to move a muscle. *I had been a good daughter and a decent sister, but a wife? Could I fulfill the expectations Michael had of me, or would I fail miserably? When he discovers the innocent child that dwells within me, will he still love me? Would my inhibitions and modesty deter me from being truly intimate with my husband?*

Suddenly, Maria called to me from downstairs. "Miss Annie, come down for breakfast, you have much to do today, young lady."

I was thankfully shaken from the worrisome concerns of my own insecurities and replied, "I'll be right down Maria, as soon as I wash up." Having been born and raised in "West-by-God Virginia," I had always pronounced wash-as "warsh,"-and had unfortunately been teased for it ever since I moved to Buffalo. When I finished in the bathroom, I proceeded across my bedroom, opened my chifferobe, and gazed at my exquisite wedding dress. *How beautiful my dress was*! I thought to myself. Now teeming with excitement instead of fear, I looked forward to this day's event. The nausea in the pit of my stomach had now turned into hunger pains. *Everything will be just fine, I love Michael and he loves me. How can that be frightening?* I said to myself as I glided wistfully down the staircase.

"My goodness Annie, you're still in your nightgown and robe? You have so much to do today!" Aunt Bess said as she scurried past me.

"I know, I know!" I said.

The house was filled to capacity with florists and decorators bustling to and fro. Bouquets of beautiful pink and white carnations were being attached to the stair railings and two gigantic vases of white calla lilies adorned the bottom step of the staircase. Streams of shiny white satin ribbon cascaded throughout the spindles of the railings and were hanging in soft loops above each doorway. "Everything looks absolutely lovely, Aunt Bess," I said.

"Well then, Missy, after you eat your breakfast, you better start looking lovely as well," Aunt Bess said in her usual "take charge," articulate voice.

I reached the kitchen just as the flapjacks and bacon were being served. All my siblings were gathered around the table and, much to my surprise, already dressed in their wedding attire. "Good lord, what time is it?" I asked.

"Well, my lady, it's half past eleven," Frank replied sarcastically. "Aunt Bess said we were to let you sleep in a bit."

"Yes, you need extra sleep today, because you won't git any tonight," James stated teasingly. Then the whole family started laughing while I, of course, blushed profusely.

"You'd better hurry, Annie," Lizzy said. "Your hairdresser and manicurist will be here soon."

"Oh, heavens, I don't understand all this fuss," I said while diving into the flapjacks and bacon.

"This is your wedding day, after all. Don't you want to look beautiful for Michael?" Aunt Bess said as she spun around the kitchen, grabbing only a cup of coffee.

"Yes, Auntie, of course I do." Again, I blushed.

It was now twelve o'clock! We all had to be at Saint Marks' Church by 12:45, since the ceremony was scheduled to begin at 1:00 p.m., sharp! My nails had been polished. My hair had been expertly and skillfully coiffed. Now was the time for my loving aunt to assist me with my wedding dress. As she pulled this gown of white taffeta, covered in lace and beading, over my head, I started to think of Momma. *How she would have loved this day. Papa too! He would have been beaming with pride.* Sensing my melancholy, Aunt Bess said, "I'm sure your momma and papa are looking down from heaven."

I am sure Momma could never have dreamed of such a day for me, since she and Papa only had a civil ceremony at the Justice of the Peace in Weston. She told me that the only attendant at their wedding had been Aunt Bess as a witness. After their civil ceremony, Gramma and Grampa had a little "shin-dig" for them at the house in celebration of their getting married. A handful of relatives and friends came to the house and enjoyed some of Gramma's fine cooking. They, of course, did not have any money to go on a honeymoon trip, so they spent their first wedding night right there in Gramma's house- the same house where they would spend the rest of their lives together.

Michael had told me that he had plans for our honeymoon, but refused to discuss them with me. He said he wanted it to be a surprise! I did not really care where we going, only that we would be alone together. ALONE! The butterflies were back and my fear was again intensifying.

"Let's get this show on the road," I said, trying not to show my nervousness.

As I descended the staircase, the entire family assembled in the foyer gasped. Roy said, "Annie, you're a sight for sore eyes!"

Chapter 13

The wedding ceremony went on without a hitch! (I guess I should say with a hitch, since Michael and I got "hitched," as they say in West Virginia.) Sarah was the flower girl and looked so sweet in her knee-high, white, lacey dress. She tossed pink rose petals from her basket as she marched down the aisle. Jacob, dressed handsomely in a miniature sized blue tuxedo, was the ring bearer. He carried our gold wedding rings on a white satin pillow as if he were transporting two raw eggs from our old chicken coop. Lizzy and Janey were my bridesmaids, wearing floor-length, pink taffeta gowns with matching ribbons in their hair. Since Michael was an only child, he had requested that James and Roy stand up as his groomsmen. Frank, being the musical genius of the family, was the pianist, as well as the soloist for the ceremony. He sang the beautiful parlor song entitled "I Love You Truly" in his sweet baritone voice. My brothers were so handsome in their blue tuxedos, white shirts, and blue bowties, that it astounded me. I was so proud of them all.

When I proceeded down the aisle, Michael's eyes met mine. Time and space stood still, and it seemed as if nothing else mattered in the world. He looked so debonair in his sailor's dress blues, which I had asked him to wear. He fought me at first, saying he wanted to look like the groomsmen, but my wishes prevailed. I felt a little saddened that my papa was not here to walk me down the aisle and give me away.

However, as soon as I reached the altar, Michael took my hand and all was right with the world.

At the end of the ceremony, which seemed to only last a few moments, we declared our vows to each other and exchanged rings. Michael then lifted my veil and kissed me ever so softly. I could feel the love that emanated between us. I knew that this man, my husband, would be my love forever. Sensing my sadness over my parents not being with me today, he leaned over and said, "Annie, my wife, I will always be at your side and will never leave you. I'll love you forever."

Once the priest introduced us as man and wife, we turned to greet our congregation of family and friends. As they stood and cheered, I noticed Aunt Bess was still in her seat. She looked very tired and her face was as pale as a ghost. She was crying into her white-gloved hands. We started the march down the aisle, but stopped at my dear aunt's seat and presented her with a single pink rose from my bridal bouquet. "Aunt Bess, thank you for this magnificent wedding. We both love you very much," we said to her in unison.

We stood together, Michael and I, with our wedding party, at the far end of the church near the doorway. Everyone that marched by us shook our hands, gave us hugs, and passed on their good wishes for a wonderful married life. After about the tenth person, I discreetly bent down, lifted my dress a bit and slipped off my shoes. "You can take the girl out of the country, but you can't take the country out of the girl," Michael whispered into my ear. Once the congregation had left the church, Michael and I thanked the priest and slowly proceeded to the outdoors where the anticipating crowd began to shower handfuls of rice upon us. As Michael helped me into his car, I noticed Aunt Bess standing on the sidelines. She was still crying. "We'll see you at the house for the reception," Michael cried out. My concern for Aunt Bess became foremost in my mind. *Does she fear she will be left alone one day? I must reassure her that we all will be together, forever.*

Michael's car led the motorcade from the church to Aunt Bess's house. He insisted he drive the two of us to the house in order to spend a few quiet moments alone with me. "Annie, since it is December and very cold, I planned for us to spend our honeymoon in Florida. We will stay at the Ford Hotel tonight and tomorrow evening get on a flight to Tampa. How does that sound to you?"

"Oh, Michael, that sounds wonderful!" I replied as I kissed him on the cheek. "I'm so sick of this cold, snowy weather. It will be delightful to bask in the sun for a few days!"

We reached Aunt Bess's and before I could reach for the door handle, Michael leaned over and kissed me passionately. I felt my whole body go completely weak. I no longer was frightened of the passion and the intimacy that we would experience as a couple on this blessed night—our wedding night! I was actually looking forward to spending an undisturbed, serene evening alone with Michael.

Even though only our closest friends and family were invited to the home of my dear aunt, it was filled to capacity. Michael's friends and family, my friends and co-workers and all the neighbors that lived nearby were enjoying the food and drink provided. Maria had generously prepared a lavish after-wedding buffet dinner. There were several types of meat and fish, large bowls of fresh green salads and succulent fruits of the season. For the highlight of the dinner, the local bakery had created the most magnificent four-tiered, rose-covered wedding cake. Michael and I sliced our exquisite cake together and then served it to our guests. Aunt Bess had engaged a five-string quartet to play soothing melodies during the reception. Michael and I danced the traditional first waltz and I felt like a floating princess as my new husband twirled me around the floor. We then toasted our endearing wedding party and our delightful guests with pink, bubbly champagne. As is the tradition, I positioned myself at the top of the staircase and threw the bridal bouquet. To my surprise, our little Sarah caught it, which excited her beyond words. Before bidding them all farewell, I went upstairs to change into my traveling trousseau and stopped at Aunt Bess's bedroom. She had retired to her room shortly after she had returned from the church. My assumption was that this entire wedding preparation had been too strenuous for her.

"Aunt Bess, aren't you feeling well?" I asked, as I sat down on the bed beside her.

"Yes, my dear child, I'm just fine. I'm just a little tired," she replied with a strained voice.

"But, Aunt, you looked so pale. Can I get you anything?" I asked.

"Oh, no thank you, Annie. I just need to rest for a little while before I go back to our guests," she replied.

"No, no, no, you stay right here! Mr. and Mrs. O'Connor have taken over as the host and hostess, and I believe they are enjoying their new role. I'm sure they can handle everything quite well," I insisted.

Just then, Michael knocked on the open door. "Aunt Bess, thank you for such a wonderful wedding that you created for Annie and me."

"Come here, my son. Come closer. I want you to promise me that you'll take good care of my Annie." Aunt Bess motioned to Michael.

"You know I will, Aunt Bess. She is not only my wife now; she is the eternal love of my life." Michael smiled at me. "Annie, please hurry and change. We have a honeymoon to start."

"Aunt Bess, we will be leaving shortly for the Ford Hotel. Tomorrow evening, we will be flying to Tampa, Florida for our honeymoon. Isn't that wonderful?" I said.

"Yes, indeed. It will be great to get out of this cold and into such a warm, exciting place. Go now and change! Don't forget to pack your summer wardrobe, Annie," she said in her usual officious manner.

I kissed her cheek gently and went directly to my room to change. After I left her room, I could hear her talking with Michael. Unfortunately, she spoke in such whispered tones that I could barely hear what she was saying to him. "Michael," she began, "I want you to be tolerant and understanding of my sweet, innocent niece. She is naïve and pure. Just remember that patience is a virtue and will reap its own reward."

"I understand what you are telling me, Bess, and you needn't worry. I will be as patient and gentle as she needs me to be," Michael said as he gently kissed Aunt Bess on the forehead. My concern for my aunt was growing. I realized that she had over-extended herself for this wedding, but she seemed unusually exhausted and particularly fragile at this point. I wanted to believe, however, that with a little rest, she would be back to her old self again soon.

I collected my things, changed out of my wedding attire, and went back to Aunt Bess's room where Michael was still sitting by her side. "I'm ready, Michael!" He leaped to his feet and took my arm. "I love you, Aunt Bess. We'll see you soon," I said.

Michael and I then raced downstairs to say goodbye to all our friends and family. Michael's mom and dad hugged us both and told us to call as soon as we got to Florida. My sisters and brothers gathered around the two of us and brandished us with hugs and kisses. Lizzy started to cry, as usual, but I said, "Lizzy, we'll be back in a week because *my husband* has to report back to training camp." Everyone followed us to the door and waved goodbye as we stepped off the porch.

Even though it was very cold and snowing heavily, I took a moment to enjoy the beautiful winter scene before me. In the twilight, I noticed the street before us was covered with at least a foot of snow. The dimly lit streetlights were glowing delicately over the snow, making it sparkle. Each limb of every apple tree that lined the sidewalks was finely dusted with snow. It looked as if God himself had sprinkled powdered sugar from the heavens above over all the trees. At this time of the evening, the city was at last peaceful and calm. It looked pure and clean with the new fallen snow.

"Hurry, Annie. You'll get soaking wet in this snow," Michael beckoned.

"I'm coming; I just wanted to take in this winter wonderland," I said.

We reached the Ford Hotel in a flash. *I guess my husband*

was in a bit of a hurry, I thought to myself, again blushing. The bedroom he had reserved for us was incredibly opulent, with satin curtains and a huge chandelier, adorned with crystals, hanging from the center of its high ceiling. Yes, bedroom! For the room had only a dresser, a closet and very large, pretentious-looking bed—the bed that Michael and I would be sharing for the duration of this night—our wedding night!

Butterflies returned to my stomach and my heart was pounding nearly out of my chest. I could hardly move. Michael approached my frozen body, put his arms around me and said, "Annie, don't be afraid. I love you very much and I will never do anything to hurt you." He then kissed me so warmly and gently that I surrendered my whole being to him.

Chapter 14

December 7, 1941

I arose a little before 8:00 a.m. with a feeling of sensual contentment and a smile upon my face. When I walked to the window of our suite, I was astonished to see how much snow had fallen throughout the night. The people that were out shoveling their sidewalks seemed to be up to their hips in snow. I started to worry that our flight might be delayed or even canceled. As I contemplated the week ahead of us, I began to daydream about sunny Florida and could almost visualize the warm, sandy beaches and the crystal clear blue waters. A whole week alone with Michael—how wonderful married life can be. I experienced total fulfillment and finally realized that the intimacy I shared with Michael was the one thing I had longed for all my life. The wall I had used as a shield from emotional involvement these past few years had fallen and I suddenly had sensed an absolute contentment within myself.

"I never thought you were an early riser, Annie," Michael said. He came up behind me and put his strong arms around me. "Come back to bed, my love. We have the whole day before our flight leaves."

"With all this snow, Michael, do you think our flight will be canceled?" I asked.

"I doubt it, but I'll call the airport in a few hours to find out for sure," he replied.

We went back to our honeymoon bed and snuggled together for warmth, and fell peacefully into a blissful sleep.

A few hours later, I awoke again and exclaimed, "I'm starving! Let's call room service and get breakfast."

"Yes, I'm getting hungry as well. Tell them I want bacon and eggs with toast," Michael demanded.

"Hold on there a minute. You're the man of this family. You are supposed to hunt it and then I cook it," I said jokingly.

As he chuckled to himself, he went to the in-house phone and called room service. I again strolled to the window to check the weather. "Oh, my goodness, there are people rushing around everywhere—and this is Sunday. I wonder what's going on. Come over here and look for yourself, Michael."

"That's odd. Sunday is usually the most peaceful day of the week in this hectic city. Besides that, almost everyone should be in church at this time of day." A knock on our door startled us, and then Michael said, "Oh, that's probably room service."

"So quickly?" I asked.

When Michael opened the door, a uniformed gentleman handed him a telegraph wire and held out his hand for a tip. Michael's jaw dropped as he read the wire. "It's from my commanding officer. I am to report to the Norfolk Naval Station immediately."

"What? It must be a joke. Why in the world would he make you do that? After all, you're on your honeymoon," I stated irately.

The gentleman at the door said in astonishment, "Haven't you heard?"

"Heard what?" I asked.

"It came over the radio a little bit ago: **Japan bombed Pearl Harbor!**"

"Oh, my God!" Michael and I said in unison.

After tipping the gentlemen, we shut the door and just looked at each other for a few moments. I felt panic run through my veins like ice water. A shiver went up my spine and I began to cry. The Navy is taking my husband away from me on our second day of wedded bliss. They can't do this to us! Michael can't leave me—not now! He is a part of me and I am a part of him. Michael looked as white as a ghost, but promptly dressed in his sailor's uniform. He scurried to the window to observe the signs of prevailing confusion. People were running about as if the sky were falling, not knowing which way to turn.

"Annie, get dressed. We'll go down to the lobby to see what's happening," Michael said.

I wiped the tears from my eyes and dutifully followed my husband's directions, even though I wanted to lock both of us up in this beautiful room and never leave. When we reached the main floor and the elevator doors opened, a world of panic and madness surrounded us. Women and children were crying. Men were rushing back and forth from radio to radio trying to hear the latest news. Michael spotted a group of sailors at the front desk. He approached them and asked where they were heading. All of them replied that they had been reassigned to Norfolk. Some of these sailors had been on leave from boot camp in the Great Lakes, just as Michael had been. I started to recognize a look of eagerness coursing through them, almost as if they were anxious to go to war. *How ridiculous*! I thought. Then I saw Michael's face as he turned towards me. This must be a masculine reaction, for Michael seemed to have this same *ridiculous* sense of enthusiasm flowing through his own manly disposition.

"Annie, I'm so sorry, but duty calls. I have to go to the airport with these other sailors and catch a flight to Norfolk in thirty minutes," Michael said.

"Michael, you can't leave!" I said, as I again burst into tears.

"You know I have to, my love. I have just enough time to take you back to Aunt Bess's and then stop to say goodbye to my mother and father."

"Oh, Michael. At least let me go with you to the airport," I pleaded.

"No, I don't want to leave you alone at the airport. I'm taking you home where you can be with your family. One of my buddies over there said he'd picked me up at my house and we all can go to the airport together," Michael said.

If I hadn't known better, I would swear Michael sounded surprisingly excited. I could see it in his eyes: a look of revenge towards the enemy who had committed this atrocity against our country. On the way to Aunt Bess's house, we barely spoke to each other. I just hung on to Michael's arm for dear life, hoping beyond hope that I could keep him by my side. All we could say to each other was that we loved one another. Michael kept promising that he would not be gone for long and that when he returned, we would go on our Florida honeymoon.

"I don't care about any stupid honeymoon. I don't want you to leave!" I begged.

"I know, Annie, but the country needs every trained soldier and sailor to fight for our democracy. I can't believe the Japanese bombed Hawaii without any warning. That's dirty fighting. Well, they'll get as good as they gave, and more!" Even though I thought he was being irrational, I could see the fervor build within him.

When we reached the house, Aunt Bess and all my siblings ran out the front door. "Michael, your parents called and told us you had to go to Norfolk. Isn't what the Japanese did a horrible thing? When do you have to go? What about your honeymoon?"

Aunt Bess asked a million questions as she hurried us into the house.

Enjoying the sanctity of familiar surroundings, I replied, "Aunt Bess, Michael can't stay here long. He has only thirty minutes before his flight to Norfolk leaves, and he wants to say goodbye to his family."

"Michael, God be with you," Aunt Bess said as she kissed him on the cheek.

"Knock them Japanese dead!" James said. Then the whole family gave Michael a hug goodbye and told him they would take good care of his wife.

Michael and I walked back outside and stood on the porch to say our goodbyes. "I will write to you as soon as I can. I'm not sure, but one of my sailor buddies thinks that once we get to Norfolk we will be assigned to the *USS Yorktown* and be deployed to the South Pacific," he said.

"The *Yorktown* is an aircraft carrier, isn't it?" I asked.

"Yes, she is one of the finest and safest ships in the Naval Fleet. Please don't worry about me; I'll be fine. Just remember how much I love you." Michael kissed me softly and held me in his arms. Before I could say anything, he walked down the steps and into his car. As he pulled away, I said, "I'll love you, forever."

Even though the snow was waist high and the temperature had plummeted into the single digits, I patiently stood on the front porch steps waiting for Michael's plane to go overhead. *"Please God, hear my prayer. Keep Michael out of harm's way and return him to me safe and sound."*

Chapter 15

Local newspapers reported the *USS Yorktown* discontinued its convoy duty in the Atlantic and docked in Norfolk, Virginia to ready the ship for deployment to the Pacific. The re-fueled and re-manned aircraft carrier left Norfolk on December 16, 1941. The newspapers also had reported that on December 11, 1941, Germany had declared war on the United States.

Not only were our men and women of the armed forces fighting a war against the incomprehensible Japanese, but they were also fighting a war against Hitler's abysmal Nazi troops. I told myself I should not read the newspapers because the news always upset me. Nevertheless, every day, I would be one of the first at the newsstand, waiting for the papers.

I had not heard anything from Michael for more than a month. Then, on January 10, 1942, I received a letter from Michael stating that his ship, the *Yorktown*, had arrived in San Diego, California on December 30. His ship had become the flagship for Rear Admiral Fletcher's newly formed Task Force 17. "Our first mission," his letter read, "is to escort a convoy carrying Marine reinforcements to Samoa. We will be departing San Diego on January 6, 1942." He reported that he was in good health and actually enjoyed being on board ship. He said, "They keep us very busy every day, cleaning the guns and swabbing the decks." The end of the letter brought me to tears. It read:

> Annie, I think about you every minute of my day. I think about our wedding night and I remember how beautiful you were. I close my eyes and I see the shape of your body and remember the smoothness of your skin. I miss the smell of your hair and the softness of your lips. Sometimes when I think of our lovemaking and how closely we felt, I feel as if I might go mad. I cannot bear being apart from you. Just one night with you was not enough. I want to spend the rest of my life lying next to you and feeling as one. He ended his letter, I'll love you, forever!

With Michael stationed on the aircraft carrier *Yorktown*, all mail sent to him went through a central post office. I would write to him almost every day, but I do not think he was receiving my letters. I would receive one, maybe two letters from him a month, but his responses were always quite vague. I continually read the daily papers and listened to news broadcasts on the radio for war updates.

It was reported that the *Yorktown* came in to Pearl Harbor for replenishment, and then was back out to sea on February 14, 1942. She was bound for the Coral Sea where she resumed patrols until April, staying out of reach of Japanese land-based aircraft but ready to carry out offensive operations whenever necessary. Once the situation in the South Pacific seemed stabilized, the *Yorktown* put in to the harbor at the Tonga Islands for needed upkeep. There were indications that the Japanese intended to make a seaborne attack in the first week of May; the *Yorktown* again headed for the Coral Sea on April 27.

Whenever the *Yorktown* was mentioned in the news, I would listen intently, thinking about Michael and what he was going through on the ship. He had told me that he was a gunner's mate and it was his job to make sure his guns were at the ready for any incoming Japanese planes. Not only was his ship threatened by air attacks; the Japanese launched torpedoes from their submarines as well. In one of his letters, he told me that one evening, three Japanese planes mistook the *Yorktown* for one of their own carriers and tried to land on her. Our gunfire drove them off; they crossed our bow and then turned away out of range. Then, just twenty minutes later, more enemy pilots made the same mistake, but this time we gunned one of them down into the sea.

The following day I heard on the news that the *Yorktown* had dodged eight torpedoes, but from the air; they were attacked by a Japanese plane. The *Yorktown* had managed to evade all but one bomb. That bomb had penetrated the flight deck and exploded below decks, killing or seriously injuring nearly sixty-six men. I was devastated. That whole week after hearing that news, I was sick. I couldn't eat! I couldn't sleep! I was a total mess! I convinced myself that Michael was one of those sixty-six men. I waited pensively each day for a report from the War Department telling me of Michael's certain demise.

On Monday of the following week, a letter finally came from Michael. He was alive! His letter recounted the horrible attack and told of the devastating inferno that ensued below deck. One of his friends had been horribly burned. "We have sustained a great deal of damage to the ship and are headed back to Pearl Harbor." Indeed, news reported the *Yorktown* arrived at Pearl Harbor on May 27 for repairs.

"Annie, must you cling to that radio night and day?" Aunt Bess asked with concern for my well-being. "You know the news only upsets you. You will inevitably end up sick. Then what good will you be to Michael when he comes home? Please, for your own sake, get back to work and to living your life."

I knew that I spent an excessive amount of time involved in this dreadful war, but I was absolutely consumed with worry over the well-being of my husband. My concentrated thoughts were only for his welfare. I could think of nothing else but the dire situation in which my poor husband found himself. If only I could have persuaded him against going into the Navy. I only know that if anything were to happen to Michael, well, I simply would not want to live any longer. However, I knew my aunt was right.

Ever since the wedding, Aunt Bess had been feeling poorly. She had gone to the doctor's and they had told her she just needed to take it easy for a while. I agreed to go back to work and take care of the business if she would agree to start taking care of herself. My siblings were now mature enough to help at the house and to make sure Aunt Bess maintained a more sedentary life. I, therefore, dove into the business of running our ship building industry. The war had dictated the enormous success of our company and we could hardly keep up with demand. Roy, now two years away from graduating college, promised that he would help me run the family's company. I looked forward to that day with great anticipation, for it had become quite strenuous for me. Janey, now out of high school, had planned on becoming a nurse. Unfortunately, her plans were now delayed with her announcement to me that she was in love and wanted to get married. "Janey, you're only nineteen and have your whole life ahead of you. Why do you want to get tied down?" I had once said to her.

"But, Annie, I'm in love. All I want from life is to be a wife and a mother," she replied.

That was that! Her boyfriend from high school had enlisted in the Army, so they decided on just a civil ceremony before he left. Aunt Bess and I both were disappointed, but what can you do when young people are in love? Janey asked me to stand up for them at the Justice of the Peace's Office in downtown Buffalo. The following day, Tommy, Janey's husband, left for the Army, and Janey came back to live with Aunt Bess and the rest of us. James and Frank, now eighteen and sixteen respectively, talked of nothing more than the war. "I'm going to enlist as soon as I graduate!" James told me emphatically. Then Frank stated he would be doing the same. What was it with these strong-willed, stubborn siblings of mine?

"They all take after you, Annie! When you set your mind to something, nothing or nobody can dissuade you," Aunt Bess reminded me.

"You're right, Aunt Bess, but at least I have three young'ins who still respect my opinions," I said in my best West Virginian slang.

"For now, maybe, but someday they will have their own ideas too!" Aunt Bess said.

Chapter 16

Shortly after Michael left for the state of Virginia in December of last year, our little Sarah, now thirteen, had become gravely ill. At first, we thought it was just influenza or a simple cold, but as the weeks and months passed by, her health declined. She had always been the smallest of the children in stature and quite delicate, but she seemed more frail now and weakened. Soon, Sarah began having night sweats and running fevers. She complained of headaches, feeling tired, and a loss of appetite. Aunt Bess and I had also begun to see bruising on different parts of her body, such as her arms, legs, and stomach. However, it was not until her gums started to bleed, that we took her to the hospital. The doctors were not sure what was wrong with Sarah, even after they put her through a battery of tests. It broke my heart to see my sweet little sister being poked and prodded as if she were a pincushion.

The doctors in Buffalo had requested a blood specialist from New York City to come and examine Sarah. The only diagnosis they had so far was that Sarah had a severe case of anemia. So again, the specialist ordered another battery of tests to be done. He concurred that she was indeed anemic but had found that Sarah's bone marrow was producing an exorbitant amount of abnormal white blood cells. They told us that these abnormal cells were growing faster and crowding out her normal blood cells, causing bleeding and infections.

The specialist from New York came into Sarah's room one afternoon and asked Aunt Bess and me, "Can I see the two of you in private?"

"Yes, of course," Aunt Bess replied. I, on the other hand, noticing the grim look upon his face, wasn't sure I wanted to hear what he had to say. However, we both followed him to a small waiting room down the hall from Sarah's hospital room.

"I'm sorry to tell you that Sarah has an acute form of Leukemia. Leukemia," he explained, "is a cancer of the blood cells. It starts in the bone marrow and spreads to other organs, and in this case, quite rapidly. We also found a swelling in Sarah's belly that is caused by her swollen spleen. Her lymph nodes are also swollen, which is causing her a great deal of pain. I'm afraid to say that our prognosis is not good."

"What do you mean by 'not good'? Can't you do anything for her?" I screamed at the doctor. Once I had heard the word "cancer," my brain shut down and all reason went out the window. "You're a specialist; that's why they brought you here. You have to do something!" I shouted.

"Well, there is something new," the doctor said. "There is a new procedure, but it is only experimental at this stage. It is a treatment using a newly founded nitrogen mustard chemical developed by the United States Army. The treatment is called chemotherapy."

"Then, by all means, you must do it. You must treat her with these chemicals. I will not lose another person to cancer," I pleaded.

"You both need to know that there are no guarantees. As I said, this is a new field into which the medical community has been delving, and we don't know what all the side effects will be. We do know that the chemical agent we inject into Sarah's body will destroy those cells that divide rapidly, as with cancer cells. However, we know too that there are certain normal cells that also divide faster than others. We suspect these faster dividing normal cells may also be destroyed during chemotherapy. These include the cells of the intestinal tract, bone marrow, and hair follicles. There is a possibility that chemotherapy may exhibit certain side effects like nausea, vomiting, and hair loss."

"If Sarah doesn't get this chemotherapy, how long does she have, doctor?" Aunt Bess asked quietly.

"There is no way to be sure, but I would say from approximately three months to maybe a year," the doctor replied.

"How soon can you start this treatment?" Aunt Bess asked.

"As soon as possible; I'll contact the other doctors and we'll work up the details."

With that, the doctor escorted us out of the waiting room and told us that by tomorrow afternoon, Sarah would be getting her first treatment.

Before we left the hospital, we stopped in to see Sarah. She was lying in that cold, uninviting bed, looking so tiny and helpless. I wanted to break down and cry, but I knew I couldn't upset her. "So, my sweet Sarah, it looks like you get to stay here and be waited on hand and foot for a while. Promise me you will eat all the supper they bring you, so you can get stronger," I said.

"I don't want to stay here alone, Annie. Please take me home with you. I can get better and stronger at home, I promise," Sarah pleaded with me, as a tear came to her eye.

"Sarah, don't cry honey. I'll stay with you. We will eat supper together and I will sleep here in this chair next to you. OK?" I knew I couldn't leave her alone. She was my baby sister and she needed me.

Aunt Bess said goodnight to us both, and went home to tell the family of Sarah's illness. I did not envy the job ahead of her; it would be devastating to the whole family. I stayed with Sarah all night long. She awoke several times during the night crying in pain. The nurses would bring in pain medication for her and she would doze off to sleep once again. It seemed she was either in excruciating pain or in a semi-comatose state, which became unbearable for me to watch. I prayed that evening for Sarah and asked God to make the treatment she would receive a success. I also prayed to God to watch over

Michael and to send him home to me. I needed him now, more than ever.

I finally fell asleep with my head on the side of Sarah's bed and my hand holding hers. I dreamed of sailing on the *Annie* out onto the sea. The waters were an azure blue and the waves had tips of white foam that looked like boiled frosting. Dolphins were swimming alongside of my ship as the moonshine danced across my bow. The feeling of a warm, salty breeze drifted upon my face. There was nothing between me and the world around me. Nothing but the wind and the sea.

Morning and reality came all too soon. I heard Sarah whimpering softly. "What's wrong, sweetie?" I asked quietly.

"I hurt all over, Annie. Why don't they do something?" Sarah's cracked voice broke my heart.

"They are going to give you some new medicine today. It won't be long now. Please stay strong for me," I answered.

"I will, Annie," Sarah whispered quietly.

Aunt Bess had brought the rest of my family to the hospital to be with Sarah during her first treatment. I could see in their eyes that they had spent the entire night crying, but they all put on a fake smile for their beloved sister Sarah. She was happy to see them as they hugged her one by one. At 2:30 p.m., the doctors and nurses came into Sarah's room and wheeled her bed down the hall into a laboratory. Although Aunt Bess and I were the only two allowed in the lab with Sarah, Roy and the rest of the children stood outside in the hallway during the whole procedure, staring in through the window of the door. They inserted an IV into Sarah's tiny arm and administered the chemicals that were supposed to kill the cancerous leukemia cells. The treatment lasted almost an hour, and then she was taken back to her room. Almost immediately, Sarah's poor little body started to quiver as she experienced a reaction to the chemotherapy. The doctor explained to us that while the chemicals destroyed the cancerous cells, they also would destroy healthy cells. They also said that we could expect Sarah to get worse before she got better.

She did indeed: her condition got much worse. In the

ensuing weeks of the chemotherapy treatments, she became violently ill with vomiting and pain. She started losing her hair by clumps and the color of skin became a putrid grey. She pleaded with me everyday to stop these treatments. "I can't stand this any more. I want to die and be with Momma and Papa," she begged.

I kept hoping and praying these treatments would kill the cancer and cure her, but I was beginning to believe that they were killing my sweet Sarah instead. Each day I could see the sickness killing her spirit, killing her joy for life, killing her sweet nature. I could no longer watch this horrible disease, and even more, the horrific treatments she had to endure, destroy my sweet, gentle baby sister. I begged the doctors to try something else—something not so harsh—but, they said there wasn't anything else available to them. I felt as if we were punishing our sweet, innocent Sarah by putting her through those excruciating treatments. Aunt Bess and I took turns staying with Sarah during the following three weeks. We watched our precious Sarah retreat into nothing but a shell of a girl. Her tiny, bald head became the frame for a sallow, gaunt face with eyes that were sunken and dim. We saw the light of life disappear from those once beautiful, big brown eyes. We witnessed her body shrivel into a skeletal state as cancer ate away at her very soul. We questioned God's decision in bestowing one of his children with this outrageous disease. Every day we prayed to God to give her strength. Every day Sarah pleaded with us to make it stop!

After talking with Aunt Bess, together we made the agonizing and heartbreaking decision to discontinue the chemotherapy treatments. We could no longer watch her body be ravaged by cancer. We could no longer watch, as her pain continued to escalate. Aunt Bess and I set up a meeting with the doctor to discuss what other measures could be taken to help our little Sarah. We told him emphatically that we wanted to stop the chemical treatments that were being given to her. We said we would pray to God for her unfettered survival.

When we went to Sarah's room to tell her she would no

longer have to endure these terrible treatments, we found we were too late. Sarah had breathed her last breath just as we entered her room. She looked up at us and smiled. Then she was gone.

We would like to believe that she was smiling because she knew she was going to be with Momma and Papa.

Chapter 17

The days following Sarah's funeral were the most heartbreaking days of our lives. We all missed her running about the house, playing hide 'n' seek with her little brother Jacob. We missed her sunny disposition and all the jokes she played on her brothers and sisters. Even though she had always been frail, she was so full of life that she brightened everyone's day. Aunt Bess took Sarah's death the hardest. Since she had not been feeling well herself, Sarah's death was a tremendous blow to her. Shortly after the funeral, Aunt Bess had taken to her bed. She said it was not natural to have one of her children die before she did. Aunt Bess had long since felt herself to be a real mother to this orphaned family and called each one of us-her child. My dear aunt stopped eating and refused to come out of her bedroom. She seemed even worse than when Uncle Charlie died. "Why did God let this happen?" she would ask. "Why did he take someone so young? Why didn't he take me instead?"

Despite all of our pleas, Aunt Bess continued to close herself off to the world. About a month after Sarah died, my beloved aunt had a massive heart attack and passed away. I believe that my uncle's death had put a crack in Aunt Bess's heart but when Sarah passed away so young, it broke my dear aunt's heart completely.

Roy went back to college to finish his studies. James and Frank dove whole-heartedly into their schoolwork. Janey took over Aunt Bess's role as care keeper of the household, and the two youngest ones, Lizzy and Jacob, wondered aimlessly from school to home, missing their sister Sarah and their Aunt Bess. As for me, I buried myself, once again, into the ship building business. I spent ten to twelve hours a day working at the office. We were making our monthly quota of warships, and making tons of money. I continued to keep aware of how the war was going by reading the daily newspapers and listening to the radio dutifully. I tried to keep Michael informed of all happenings within our household, but I was never sure he received my letters. After the news reported that the *Yorktown* had again put to sea, bound for Midway Island, I never received another letter from him.

Summer had again presented itself, with its torrid sweltering days and its cooler breezy nights. The only reprieve from the scorching heat was the fresh cooling breeze from the lake. On the weekends, I would gather my family as crew to take the *Annie* out on Lake Erie. It was mid-June and the weather had been perfect for sailing. We would set her to sail early Saturday morning and spend the whole day on the lake. Sometimes we would drop anchor in the middle of the lake, and dive off *Annie*'s bow to swim in the cool refreshing waters. We would picnic on the aft deck and talk of current events. On some occasions, we discussed our futures and our pasts. Sadness would engulf us when we talked of the loved ones we had lost. We would all cry and hug together, thanking the dear Lord that we still had each other. At dusk, we headed the *Annie* back to the shoreline and tied her up at the dock for the night. I enjoyed these times with the family on the *Annie*, but I missed the moonlight and the shimmering diamonds on the water. Some nights, when the full moon was out, I would slip down to the docks and watch the diamonds as they skipped across the water. I would look up to the heavens in hopes that Momma, Papa, Uncle Charlie, Aunt Bess, and sweet Sarah were enjoying God's handy work also. I would talk with them as if they were beside me, telling them of how the rest of their family was thriving and how mature each one of them had become. *How proud you all would be of this wonderful family of yours*! I would say to them silently. One more thing I would ask: "Please watch over Michael and Tommy during this dreadful war."

In late June, news of the *Yorktown* again filled the radio broadcasts. It was reported that the she had been hit by at least two Japanese torpedoes and was mortally wounded. She had lost power and then went dead in the water. Later in the evening, another carrier, the *Hammann,* was hit and was sunk close to the *Yorktown*. The blast of the underwater explosion had killed many of *Hammann*'s and a few of *Yorktown*'s men, who had been thrown into the water. Searches began to rescue men from the water, but darkness postponed the salvage until the following day. Many survivors were picked up, but by 7:00 a.m., the *Yorktown* turned over onto her port side and sank in 3,000 fathoms of water, her battle flags still flying. The second attempt at salvage was ended.

As I listened to this last report, I still had hope in my heart that Michael had been rescued. Michael's parents assured me that I would be notified one way or the other. One very long week later, I received a wire from the War Department.

> Dear Mrs. O'Connor,
> I am sorry to report to you that your husband,
> Gunner's Mate
> Michael J. O'Connor, is missing in action. . .

The rest of the wire was a blur; I went numb after reading that Michael was M.I.A., and fell to my knees sobbing. I called Mr. and Mrs. O'Connor immediately. They came to the house promptly. They tried to console me, but of course, they were distraught as well. We held each other for a long time and prayed. Michael's mother said, "Annie, if they say he is missing, that could mean he is still alive."

"You're right, I shouldn't give up hope," I answered, trying to convince myself that I would see Michael again.

Two years later

As the months passed into years, there was still no word from Michael. His official status remained as "missing in action." News from abroad told of the Nazis' atrocities against the Jews. Racism had raised its ugly head with the extermination of the Jewish people by the gassing, starvation, shooting and burning that began at the Auschwitz Concentration Camp. The act of this madman, Hitler, was the most unconscionable deed of butchery towards the human race that history ever had witnessed.

Reports of American troops being sent overseas to fight the fascists were received by many with applause. I, on the other hand, having a husband missing in action, and a brother-in-law on the front lines somewhere in Europe, could not honestly condone more fighting. I had, after all, two younger brothers who had nothing but revenge within their souls and wanted to be engaged with the enemy as soon as they could. I prayed every day this war would end before James and Frank could enlist. *God, please hear my prayer*! But, my faith in God was diminishing.

"I got a letter from Tommy today, Annie. He says he was injured and will be coming home soon." Janey was beaming with happiness. Since she had been missing him so desperately, I was delighted for her.

"Does he say where he is or what happened to him?" I asked.

"No, actually it doesn't even look like his writing. Maybe he had someone else write it for him. He just says that he is in an army hospital unit and that they will be flying him home soon," Janey answered.

It seemed odd to me that Tommy would not have written the letter himself, unless he was so badly injured that he could not do it, possibly having lost the use of his hands. In any case, I did not mention my concerns to Janey. There was no need to upset her at this point. Then, just a week later, early in the morning, Janey received a phone call from Tommy. "I'm in

Chicago, and I'm taking the train to Buffalo. I will arrive at the train station at 4:30 p.m. today. I love you and can't wait to see you!"

Unfortunately, my assumption regarding Tommy's physical condition was correct. Janey and I were waiting at the train station at 4:30 p.m. when Tommy's train pulled into the station. Janey ran towards the entrance gate just as Tommy stepped off the train. They both ran towards each other and embraced. Tommy's embrace employed a single arm only. Janey backed away from him abruptly and said, "Oh, Tommy what happened to your other arm?"

Sadness overcame him when he responded, "I left it at Normandy."

Chapter 18

On June 6, 1944, the largest single-day allied amphibious invasion of all time took place on the beaches of Normandy, France. As soon as Tommy's LCM (landing craft) hit the shores of Omaha Beach, it incurred massive mortar attacks. Within ten minutes of the transport ramps being lowered, most of the troops from the First Infantry Division were killed or wounded. Tommy had lost his right arm. He was one of the lucky few. He was flown back to the States on the next transport.

Life for our family returned to normal once again, or at least as normal as possible. Janey continued to take care of home and family and Tommy had started his rehabilitation therapy at the local Veterans Hospital. He learned how to write with his left hand as well as learning other common functions. He desperately tried to help whenever and wherever he could. He mostly worked around the house and the office, doing maintenance jobs or custodial work. Lizzy, now sixteen, had blossomed into a beautiful young lady. She had been looking into the nursing field and was planning to attend extended schooling when she graduated the following year. Our precocious Jacob, now twelve, would be entering high school the next year. God help his teachers, for he continued to be the mischief-maker in the family. James, who was now twenty, had been enrolled at the Buffalo University since the previous fall. Thank God, I was able to persuade him that enlisting in the

Armed Forces would not be advantageous to himself or the family. Frank, well, he was another story. He would graduate later that year from high school and I was still quarrelling with him about enlisting. My lifesaver, Roy, now twenty-three and graduated from college, had moved into the role of executive officer at the company. With Roy taking over a majority of my responsibilities, I could now relax a bit and concentrate on the design aspect of the business. I did have more time now to spend sailing. I would take the *Annie* out on the Lake as often as possible.

When Tommy had returned from the war, I had questioned him about Michael's ship, the *USS Yorktown*. He informed me that the scuttlebutt regarding the *Yorktown* was that it had sunk somewhere around the Midway Islands. He said there were many survivors who had been ordered to abandon ship before it went down. "Don't worry, Annie. If Michael is listed as MIA, there's a good chance he is still alive," Tommy said in a comforting voice.

"It's been over two years, Tommy, and I still haven't heard anything more. Wouldn't they have found him by now?" I asked.

"I don't know, Annie, but you mustn't give up hope."

Hope. I am not sure I have any hope left. I had hoped Sarah would get better. I had hoped that Aunt Bess's heart had not broken. I had hoped Momma never had cancer. I had hoped that Papa would have had the courage to go on without Momma. I had hoped that Uncle Charlie would still be making me laugh. I had hoped for a lot of things to be different in my life, but hope has now most assuredly turned into despair.

Maybe I had too much time on my hands now, but my outlook on what life brings to the table had been altered significantly. I spent more and more of my time contemplating "what should have been" instead of "what was." The phrase "what if" now consumes me. What if. . . Michael had not gone to war? We could have had a family of our own by now. What if. . . Aunt Bess had not died? I would not have sole responsibility for our company and my siblings. My mind was filled with a wave of depressive thoughts, and an uncertainty for my future. Hope no longer lived in my vocabulary. Hope no longer lived inside of me.

Today, August 26, is a delightful fall day. Although I normally enjoy this time of the year because of the exquisite crimson colors that all the trees display, I feel a profound sadness. This sadness, like a dark cloud, has overtaken my soul. Instead of feeling pleasure in the glorious spectacle of the autumn months and of anticipating the cleansing purity of the upcoming winter months, I suffer an overwhelming sense of doom and desolation. Life's simple pleasures, like watching the sun rise or the moon set, no longer conquer my attention. No longer do I delight in seeing a flock of seagulls soar over the water, or a fish leap from the water's boundary to devour a dragonfly. No longer does the sound of children playing or people laughing engage my senses. I no longer take satisfaction in other people's nor my own events or accomplishments. I have become my own nightmare, not caring nor believing in myself or anyone else.

When I was young, life seemed so simple. My family and I had very little. We had little money. We had little possessions. We only had each other. We loved each other and we loved our simple life. I may have been the only one in the family that wanted more. I had hopes and dreams for a better and brighter future. I thought money and possessions would make my life more fulfilled. Now, at the age of twenty-five, I have all the things I had ever dreamed of. I have a successful business, a grand home, and all the material things anyone could ask for, and yet, I am not happy. I have lost so many people in my life whom I loved. I would give everything I own, to have them back.

The very fact that I have lost so many loved ones in my life has become an overpowering venom. I have convinced myself that I no longer have a heart or a soul. God help me!

Where is that young, vibrant girl, whose zest for life was contagious? Where did she go? Has she been lost forever? These questions I ask of myself only to discover that the once naïve child is no longer a viable entity. The dark recesses of my mind have driven away any residual appetite for life. These past few weeks, I have discontinued my responsibilities at the office and relinquished my obligations at home. My melancholy has grown deeper and deeper, and my depressive mood has grown darker and darker.

Realizing that I may only have one chance left to sail the *Annie* before the cold weather maroons her at dry dock, I gathered a crew together for a final outing. This time, however, I chose some locals instead of my siblings. This excursion, I had decided, would indeed be my last journey on the *Annie*. We left the docks at 7:30 p.m. with the expectation that we could be in position to view the moonlight at about 9:00 p.m. The sails were hoisted and billowed in the wind. The waters were as blue as a sapphire and as smooth as glass. The tranquility of the wind and the water brought an absolute serenity to the decision I had resolved. Once underway, the crew began executing their nautical duties, while I positioned myself at *Annie*'s bow. I laid on the deck with my arms dangling overboard and felt as if I were part of this grand ship of mine. As her bow cut through the water, the brisk cool wind wafted through my hair and the gentle waves splashed across my face. Normally this experience would be exhilarating for me; however, this sensation was nothing more than a precursor for my own private decree.

Knowing that Roy was more than capable of running the little ship building business we had inherited from Uncle Charlie and Aunt Bess, and that Janey and Tommy would be unquestionably proficient at raising our siblings, I felt everything in my life was in order. I was finished as the caregiver of the family. I was astutely aware that my ultimate decision would cause my family grief, but I felt I could not continue this travesty I had called my life. I could not continue caring for loved ones and then losing them. I reached into my jacket pocket and pulled out a small revolver I had purchased several weeks ago. There was a single bullet in the chamber. I held it in my hand, contemplating my conclusion, when I noticed the full moon hanging in the darkened sky. It looked enormous and shone vividly across the water, creating magnificent diamonds on the water.

I watched the diamonds as they sparkled in the moonlight and once again prayed that all those in heaven, that I had loved and lost, were admiring this spectacle as well.

Michael, if you are up there with Momma and Papa, just know that I cannot live without you and will see you soon. I'll love you, forever, I whispered. Again, I looked at the revolver. *Do I have the courage?* I asked myself.

Just now, as I glance once more at the waters before me, I notice an obstruction in my "diamond" corridor. It is a shiny, triangular object floating directly in the moonlight's pathway. Although the object is at least a few hundred feet from the *Annie*, I can see something or someone moving on top of the object. I call back to my helmsman, "Do you see something moving out there?"

"Yes, I believe I do! What do you think it is?" he replies.

"I'm not sure, but it looks like a person waving his arms. Set a course directly into the moonlight."

As we approach the shiny object, we decide it is a piece of fuselage from an airplane. My helmsman told me that the news had reported that early yesterday, a plane headed for New York had lost an engine and went down over the Lake Ontario area. They believed all the survivors had been picked up by a commercial fishing boat. "This poor guy must have been moved by the northwesterly current. I bet he doesn't even know how far he has come."

Following the path of the diamonds on the water, we navigate closer and closer to this being. I can hear someone shouting out, "Annie, Annie." Has he recognized our ship? Or, is he calling. . . my name?

"Michael?"

"Yes, I'm here!. . . It's me, Annie!. . . It's your Michael!"

Printed in the United States
153162LV00004B/35/P

9 781608 603992